The Dimension Scales

and other stories.

Garry Abbott

Copyright © 2013 by Garry Abbott

No part of this publication may be reproduced, stored in or introduced into a retrieval system, or transmitted in any form or by any means (electronic, mechanical, photocopying, recording or otherwise), without the prior written permission of the copyright owner, except by a reviewer who may quote brief passages in a review.

This book is sold subject to the condition that it shall not, by way of trade or otherwise, be lent, resold, hired out or otherwise circulated without the author's prior consent in any form of binding or cover other than that in which it is published and without a similar condition including this condition being imposed on the subsequent purchaser.

For her trust and love. Thank you.

CONTENTS

Preface 7

The Diary of Derek Froggat, The Accidental Time-Traveller 10

Black Swarm 18

Love in the Shell 32

Cry Again Army 55

The Drawing Room 86

The Dimension Scales 89

Alex, Boudicca and Benny the Bear 95

Animals Attack: Parts I to IV 108

The Next Level 131

Newsbot Serial One 154

The Beep Next Door 164

Scalp 170

The Day the Stars Moved 190

The Voice of Strad 197

Preface

"I dreamed of moments in glass boxes, forever stretching out as far as I could see. And I was outside and in between, trapped, unable to move into the scenes."

That is a lyric from a song I wrote a few years ago. As I remember, I wrote it on a ukulele that I tucked into my suitcase and took with me on a family holiday to Spain. The song itself never 'made it' to live performance or broadcast of any kind, residing instead in my archive of unused compositions that help me to construct a working memory of life and my artistic development, a kind of melodic diary. The reason I am mentioning it here is the lyrics, and what they mean to the collection of stories you are about to read.

You see I really did dream of moments in glass boxes. The precise details fade with time, though I remember the morning I woke from it, feeling wrenched away from a deep, existential dream that overtakes reality and makes it seem a little dimmer when it returns. In this dream, I was disembodied, watching moments from my life, and other lives, playing out in glass boxes suspended in a white void. They were randomly distributed and stretched forever around me in all dimensions. I had the feeling that if I could stand outside that place and look in, it would seem like a dense material, and that to be there amongst the moments was to be like an observer in a microscopic universe, such as we see when we zoom into seemingly flat surfaces only to reveal they are like mountains and gullies, a hidden landscape.

But it wasn't the dream that inspired the stories in 'The Dimension Scales': the glass boxes just happened to become interwoven thematically as the collection developed. The void became a space I could refer to when I realised what the repercussions of the eponymous 'Dimension

Scales' might be, and how it influenced the 'possible worlds' that constitute the bulk of the collection. This introduction may make more sense once you have read on, or it may not: it is usually my desire to let you decide in such matters.

My intention with this collection has been to create a body of stand-alone stories that can be read in isolation, but that still have links to each other, some direct, some indirect, some fleeting and inconsequential, some causal and integral, some temporal, some abstract. When deciding on the order of the stories I wrote the title of each on a Post-it note and placed them on a white board. After much deliberation I decided to draw lines between each story that linked or referenced another in some way. I found that indirectly all but one story have some link (I will leave that to you to find out); of more interest, I found the glass boxes were back. Granted, they were made of paper, glue and ink, but those little rectangles with a tangle of arrows that bound them in unchangeable ways no matter how much I rearranged them were something close to what that dream was about.

Even deletion or destruction of the moments, the stories, represented now as they are in bytes and on paper, will not get rid of the lines that bind them - for me at least (not unless selective lobotomies become available on the NHS or I lose my mind). But even that would still not obliterate the moment in time, or some little part of matter that clings on unheard. So it is with these stories, and all stories, and so it is with all moments and all that links them.

But what's inside the boxes? Well, at first each idea that successfully grew into a narrative was in no way shaped by a preconceived theme or notion, other than my own attitudes and influences subconsciously evoked. It was only once a draft of each story existed and I started to consider the collection as a whole that I recognised certain themes had reared their heads. Metamorphosis and survival feature heavily. Exacerbation and social experimentation play a part, too. Identity is not far behind.

For this particular collection I owe a huge deal to such great writers as Roald Dahl, Douglas Adams, Isaac Asimov, Will Self, Martin Amis and Philip K. Dick for unwittingly setting my aspirations, and my family, friends and the whole wide, weird world for my inspiration.

I hope you enjoy reading this collection and thank you for your precious time.

Garry Abbott

The Diary of Derek Froggat, The Accidental Time-Traveller

Friday. 5th September. 1670. It has just gone dark.

Here begins the strangest and perhaps most unbelievable diary entry that I have ever written, and I guess anyone will ever read, if these words are discovered, which I should probably make sure never happens, at least not for another 342 years.

It has taken me a while to procure the means and get used to this method of writing. I find it hard to write with a biro, let alone with a sharpened feather and pot of ink. But finally they are beginning to trust me, I have as much parchment as I need, and, although I ought really to be writing here all that I can recall of the future, it is in these few quiet times of solitude they occasionally grant me that I intend to keep this official record of my time here. I have found a secret place, a loose floorboard, where I can safely store these documents; and soon enough, if I continue to convince them of my validity, I may earn the rights and privileges to my own property. All being well, I should have much, much more than that, but it is a dangerous line I am walking.

Firstly, I should say how I came to be here. There is not much to tell that I can make much sense of for you, I'm afraid. It was (or will be?) December 2012, and I was driving my car on the way to a dentist's appointment. Dentistry. I haven't thought of that before. Mint. Fluoride? Bicarbonate of soda? Remember to ask. Heaven forbid I should need any work doing while I am here. Sometime in the journey I began to feel particularly unwell. It was a sudden surge of pressure in my abdomen. At first I feared diarrhoea (how I now wish that was it) so I stopped the car. I was travelling the country lanes to avoid heading through Derby on the main roads, being rush hour, so I was surrounded by fields and dry stone walls. Although I could tell the feeling was unusual, I headed behind the *nearest wall, just in case my prognosis was correct and modesty shelter was required.*

While standing in that forlorn field, gripping my midriff, I convulsed, my abdomen involuntarily arching forwards as if a bolt of electricity had just passed through my entire body. It was just like in films about old mental institutions and their brutal practices. I dread to think what the current methods of restoring sanity are here: something duller than electricity, I fear. I stood frozen like this for some seconds, and could see emerging from roughly where my navel is a blue spinning light about the size of a bowling ball. It eventually emerged fully and spun suspended in the air before my twisted body. For some time I stood there, bent and unable to move. It seemed to be getting faster and crackled with a static charge. I could feel it in the air, just like after lightning. Like lightning, it was beautiful in its own way. Then, suddenly and without any other change to warn me, it shot back into my stomach and I fell unconscious.

When I came to I was in a forest and my car had gone, or I had gone - it was hard to tell. I was disorientated, naturally, and I walked with only the clothes I wore until I found a farmhouse. All I had in my pockets were my car keys, a lighter, some loose change, the flyer for the new dentist's practice I had been heading for, and some grotty tissues. My phone was in the car, along with my wallet. I knocked on the door of the farmhouse and was greeted by what I took to be character actors, tour guides for a museum experience of some kind. I explained my predicament, still thinking myself to have been kidnapped or suffering some mental breakdown. They listened intently, but they did not understand the meaning of many of my words. They spoke in very thick accents, but I understood them perfectly.

I have since found that whatever device has sent me here also makes it possible for me to communicate. The only problem I have is with explaining nouns that do not yet exist in this time. If I say the word 'phone', for example, they do not understand, and why should they, but I can with time and patience use constituent examples to explain the concept; once grasped, those who then learn the word will understand me. At first this quirk of language made it a lot harder for them to understand me than for me to understand them. Funnily enough, this ability also transmits itself to written words. I can read the few writings I am able to access, even if they are purportedly written in Latin, which I do not speak. Apparently also, my writing reads back to those from this time in a notably different metre and turn of phrase than I actually write.

I experimented with this for some time when I arrived at the Lord's house (I know I am skipping forwards somewhat here, but I must recall all I can about this peculiar event as it occurs to me). I found that when I wrote the word 'you' in the English I am accustomed to, they read the word 'thou', in that way I only know of through the little Shakespeare I have encountered. I asked them to write down the word as they saw it, and, sure enough, they wrote 'thou'. It appears that our interactions in speech and text are influenced some way by my very being here. The gods only know what this means, and how indeed it will influence this text should it be read in the future.

Anyway, I mu... (note from this entry – I heard the guards and had to cease – 06/09/1670)

Saturday. 6th September. It has been dark for some time now.

Apologies for my poor rendering of time. They do have clocks here, but I am not yet permitted one in this room and it seems that without access to several dozen time displays at any given point, I am quite unable to judge the hours accurately. This room! I came to the Lord's manor some weeks ago. He had heard tell of this strange man from another time, with his firebox, the flint that never failed, and his strange blue trousers. My jeans have caused quite a stir. They were less impressed by my thin polo shirt which perished after its first soaking in their noxious excuse for soapy water and being bashed to pieces by a demon washer lady with the arms of Popeye, but the jeans are made of sterner stuff! Faded a little, but still sturdy, and I've been allowed to keep them, despite the obvious coveting from some of the squires. I'm not sure exactly what constitutes denim; however, it could help my cause if I did, but I'll get onto that.

I was brought here by my first hosts at the farmhouse, and here I stay, until such time as the Lord is satisfied by my 'outlandish' claims. He believes my strange words, clothes and the lighter I had with me to be devices of some foreign enemy - the Dutch, I think. Sir Stanley is his name. He is an Earl and a Lord. I don't know the difference. I just call him 'my Lord', and he seems happy enough.

Although suspicious, the Lord is also either amused or curious about my predicament, and has charged me with setting down all I know and can remember of my time, along with demonstrations that can prove my memories' worth. This I have found a hard task. The lighter is temporary, and I doubt I could replicate anything of it. In my time I was an accountant. Of little use to me now. If the Lord were at all interested in double entry ledger balances I would be made a Duke or something. My general ignorance of this time does not help. I can no more make predictions about the future of any worth to these people than explain the plastic of my disposable lighter.

I have, however, found small amusements to buy myself time while I rack my brains to avoid my body being put on one. I can only presume that I will be here forever, and as such, finding favour with the Lord and perhaps even making a fortune would be a grand thing indeed. I was worried that I might cause the so-called 'butterfly' effect if I interfered, but somehow, that doesn't feel right. It is hard to explain being here, but this isn't the 'past'; for me it is the 'present', and I am here regardless. Maybe it will be like one of those films where it runs parallel. Either way, I fail to see how that is my concern at this <u>present</u> moment.

Anyway, I was talking of my small amusements. First of all, and this was a stroke of genius, the paper aeroplane! How easy to demonstrate principles of aeronautics with nothing but a folded parchment. Granted, I *have no idea how they can scale it up, but it certainly kept them amused. They have held competitions in the town, and they are a favourite amongst the children, bless the poor overworked wretches.*

The paper aeroplanes got me onto another concept, the hot-air balloon, but seeing as I am mostly required to demonstrate my own designs, I have not yet told them of this. Maybe when I have earned their respect and praise and have willing volunteers to make the flights I will tell them. I certainly wouldn't go up in a balloon designed by me! I have casually asked about methods of travelling through the air, as I don't rightly know if the balloon has yet been invented, but no one seems to understand what I am talking about.

I thought basic games would be an easy distraction but found many to already be in use, especially by some of the Lord's men who have travelled. When I revealed to the court my rough, wood-engraved 'Ludo' board with matching coloured stone pieces, one learned gent laughed and said he had seen such a game being played by foreign peasants on his travels. He may have been lying, but the Lord believed him. Not surprisingly, they are rather keen on all forms of board and card games, being devoid of radio and television. Ha! That is a concept I have found very hard to explain. It is like a box, with a glass screen, I tell them, and on that screen, I believe, are many lights that can switch on and off, or change colour. By doing this, we show many pictures, very quickly, so that they appear to move. Better still, these pictures are taken by photography, a process whereby a light-sensitive material is exposed briefly through a lens and the image on the lens is then captured, or kind of burned onto the material. 'What is this material which has such properties?' they then ask me, to which I have no answer, reaching instinctively for my internet-enabled phone which isn't there, and even if it were, would presumably not be connected. (I'm not going into the difficulty I had explaining the ethereal cloud of accessible combined knowledge that is the internet. That was a tough day.)

Anyway, I have already hit the stumbling block of creating electricity, so any inventions that require it are of little use exploring. When I tried to demonstrate the concept of static, I instinctively asked for a balloon, and then remembered about balloons. I spent some time pushing copper and zinc into a potato. I thought a lemon would be better, but they don't have them to hand here. Still, I think I got some kind of sensation from placing my tongue on the contacts, but I'm not sure that wasn't just the feeling of cold metal. Even if it were a charge, I have no idea how to turn this into a useable device. If I had a lab, the best minds of the land, all the time and resources I needed, and no other distractions (such as the possibility of having my head cut off), I may remember more. But until then, while desperation beckons, electricity is beyond me.

This is why they do not yet fully trust me. I am finding it hard to convince them that I am not just an imaginative lunatic. I need something solid I can explain and demonstrate which isn't going to kill me in the process. Otherwise my plan to succeed in this world will soon run out of steam.... Hang on!

Sunday 7th September. Definitely night-time.

Right. Apparently steam is not so revolutionary as I expected. Some of the scholars whom the Lord has now employed to examine my claims have known of the use of steam in experiments for some time. There are already published works which surpass my knowledge. It is the application that I could possibly crack, a way of converting the pressure of steam through pipes to moving parts of practical use. I think gears may help here, in order to drive a train? Regardless, that is the least of my problems. The Lord has grown impatient with me, especially following this latest failure. He wants to know of our weapons, of warfare in the 21st century. I have tried to convince him that, in our time, there is no such need for weapons, living as we do in a veritable utopia of social cooperation and a shared purpose to better humanity (I got that from Star Trek, but it sounds a nice enough idea, doesn't it?) Anyway, maybe it was obvious to him, but he did not believe me. He said, "Even if this is true, unless all war ends tomorrow, you must know the history of warfare to the point when this peace was reached?" He had a point, and pleading ignorance isn't going to work when I have made my case based on the knowledge of the world I came from (admittedly a very, very broad and shallow knowledge I am finding).

So here I am, under threat of torture and execution, required to start explaining tomorrow what I know of warfare. Of course, this won't help them so much. Even if I explained about nuclear weapons, the splitting of the atom, that is about the extent of what I know. I couldn't split an atom if one was put before me with a tiny little axe and a sign saying 'Chop Here'. But I must, I must think of something. They have gunpowder and guns. They have shown and demonstrated them to me, as much by way of a threat as a reference point. There are some easily identifiable features I could mention. The use of a cartridge or bullet case to house the gunpowder at the base of the projectile itself, rather than as a separate element. I presume that was quite a big development. I could also point out the idea of having these already loaded into a moving chamber that lines up the next projectile to the shaft by using the same force or trigger that hammers the bullet. Some rudimentary drawings of bullet and gun shapes would probably be of great worth. I have experimented with these in my desperation and am surprised at how accurately I can recall such things: it must be the influence of the movies once again. Unfortunately, in this case, I think the scholars and engineers would soon understand me on this concept, and, as a concept, does that not start the invention of mortars and heavy artillery? After all, are they not just larger guns with larger bullets?

And then there is chemical warfare. They already have a rather sound and devilish knowledge of the various noxious gases and poisons. If they coupled this with the idea of large projectiles, no matter how crude, what hell would beset this world? Maybe if I only vaguely cover the concepts it will take them just as long to figure out the practicalities as it would have done anyway? Maybe my drawings of artillery and machine-guns, which for now I shall keep secret with these documents, will be a tantalising yet ultimately unobtainable distraction for generations, and buy me time to think of something industrial that will keep their curiosity sated?

No, I could cause terrible devastation with this knowledge. I must think of something else, I must, and they can never see this, or my diagrams, even this would be enough to...

My stomach is hurting. Oh God. I can't move my body, even as I write this, I can just flex my fingers enough to scrawl but I cannot grip the page. It's the light, it's coming again. Please if you find this, destroy it. Destroy it! And the drawings, below the floorboards. You don't want to end up like the future I came from! It can be avoided! Don't do it. Hitler! Don't let anyone called Hitler anywhere near power in Germany. Don't let a Russian man, Stalin! He will kill many. 9/11! The Twin Towers, planes, bin Laden, don't let him. There were no WMDs, it was a lie. Blair, Bush. Bad things. Can't hold onto this pen. Please, I am a lunatic. Ignore it all! Except those last bits. Oh no. Here it comes again. I can hear a violin.

Black Swarm

Mark and Steve surveyed the scene. Besides the refrigerator, wedged between the plywood partition, a mountain of displaced earth rose up and back to an unseen peak, and, at its base, black forms scurried.

'That's mental,' said Steve as he kneeled down to get a closer look. 'It could be massive.'

Having ants in the house was nothing new for Mark. Most days during late spring he would come downstairs to find them carrying away breadcrumbs, sugar grains and anything else they could lay their mandibles on. They never swarmed the kitchen counter; there would just be a few, scouting, gathering, circling. He killed them, of course. It was necessary. He usually let at least one get away, hoping it would leave a chemical trail behind, warning about the dangers of coming 'topside'.

The displaced earth wasn't unusual either. A fine dust would creep out onto the red tiles from somewhere below the fridge, like a collapsed sand dune at his feet. It was easily swept away or vacuumed up. He just presumed that however they were getting in, they brought some of the earth with them.

A smell had alerted him to the problem. One of those 'something left in the fridge too long' smells, like shoes after carrying bare feet on a hot day, with added notes of rotten milk. A smell that at a distance almost reminds you of food, a blue cheese perhaps, but as you get closer it twists and congeals within your receptors. It was also a phantasm of an odour. He had checked the fridge several times, taking care to clear out anything suspicious. He found an old plum behind the microwave and carefully picked it up, fearing maggoty contents. It was misshapen, like a squashed ping-pong ball, but it was solid, and didn't reek. Eventually, in a desperate plea to locate the miasma, he resorted to checking behind the white goods, and that's when he found it.

He'd barely moved the fridge a few centimetres, shuffling it awkwardly out of the fitted cubby hole, when he saw the mountain. By moving the fridge he had exposed one side of the structure which kept its coherency and revealed a cross-section of the thin mound. It had been compacted between the fridge and partition, and ants emerged from it. Not many, just a few scouts to figure out what the hell was going on, but Mark soon replaced the fridge, fearing a retaliation should the nest crumble. The unsavoury stench moved down his priority list.

'Yeah. I mean, they don't seem to come out of there much anymore, but there it is,' Mark replied. He stood in the narrow galley kitchen, hands on hips, happy to be sharing his dilemma with his friend Steve.

'How far back does it go? It could go under the house. This might just be an annex,' said Steve, who had returned to his full height.

'No idea. But in my mind, we pull out the fridge, get the Dyson, suck it up and spray the little bastards as they pour out.'

Mark shared the house with his girlfriend Susan who was away for the weekend visiting relatives in darkest Durham. Mark had used the opportunity to invite Steve for some 'man-time' as he and Susan used to call it. Left to his own devices, Mark would have spent the weekend alone playing games, watching films, but Susan had been firm with him, responsible as she felt for his lack of social life.

'Why don't you ask Steve around? He needs a bit of company now he's on his own,' she had suggested while packing her little purple suitcase and attending to the several hundred processes she was required to follow before being able to leave the house for two nights.

'Yeah, I suppose,' Mark replied. He wasn't one to argue, and anyway, he did like seeing Steve, but wasn't so keen on getting a damp shoulder if he started talking about Mandy again and how he 'should have seen it coming'. He needed an activity to distract them from all that 'stuff'.

'I know!' Mark said, reaching for his phone, 'I'll ask him to come and give me a hand with that bloody ants' nest. Make a day of it. A few beers. Yeah.'

Susan couldn't fathom the sense of it, why men are like that. *What a funny lot,* she thought. She returned to packing while Mark rang Steve and they arranged the Great Ant Massacre of '23.

***

'So, do you want the hoover or the spray?' Mark asked.

'It's your house, dude,' said Steve, who secretly wanted the bright red spray bottle with the picture of an ant behind a crossed circle.

'Fair enough. I'll suck, you spray,' said Mark. They both laughed at the innuendo.

They had planned it pretty carefully up to this point. All the doors to the kitchen were closed and seals formed with plastic bags, just in case they swarmed beyond control. The hoover was plugged in and ready, the chamber emptied. The spray was primed. A window was opened so that they didn't get overcome by the toxic vapours.

Together, Mark and Steve wobbled the fridge out inch by inch on the rubber corner feet. They only took it as far as the power cord would allow. Steve had to hop over the top to get to the right-hand side where the nest was now revealed again. It was awkward. The kitchen was narrow and the fridge blocked the angles of approach. Mark knelt, hoover in hand, Steve leaned over him, spray at the ready. So far, despite the fridge movement, only a couple of ants had descended from the pile.

'Can you hit the power switch from there?' asked Mark, who realised he couldn't actually reach it from his crouched vantage point.

'Yeah, you ready?'

'Do it.'

The hoover whirred to life and Mark plunged it into the base of the ants' nest. The soft earth yielded easily and a steady stream glided through the pipe into the chamber. The hill started to reduce like an upturned sand timer. So far no ants. Steve held back from using the spray.

'Maybe it's not as bad as all that?' said Steve, lowering his bottle.

Mark continued, the nest diminishing. It was nearly all gone. Still no ants. Inside the hoover chamber the earth sat neatly, not even half-filling the capacity. That was it. No more sand. No more ants. Mark gestured awkwardly from his wedged position and Steve switched off the hoover.

'Is that it?' asked Steve, who couldn't see past the shuffling form of Mark trying to disengage. Mark managed to get free and stood to face Steve.

'I think so,' said Mark, who was now worried about how to spend the next hour or two. 'Let's put the fridge back – hang on...'

They looked down at their feet. All around, a black ripple was forming. The exodus had begun.

Mark and Steve jumped to battle stations. Steve laid down a volley of the toxic spray. Large sections of the black mass went still. Mark came in afterwards and started sucking up the dead, and many of the living. They kept coming, and now flying ants appeared, looking to escape and start a new colony.

'Get the fliers! Get the fliers!' screamed Mark, not wanting to turn one nest into several.

Hands and newspapers slapped against any surface the awkward aerial ants landed on. One flew into the toaster: Steve reached over and turned it on.

'Good move!' said Mark as he clapped his hands together and caught another.

The aerial battle had distracted them, however, and now the floor was a solid black as the ground troops moved out.

'Get the doors! Get the doors!' Mark ordered, and Steve hopped over the fridge to lay down a suppressing chemical trail at each exit on the far side of the kitchen.

'I'll push them your way!' he said, as the swarm fled from his poisonous perimeters.

Mark was waiting on the other side, sweeping the hoover left and right, sucking up hundreds upon hundreds of the black army. The dust chamber colour changed from sandy grey to black as it filled with POWs. On the other side of the fridge, those that could not run fast enough were sizzling and blistering from Steve's napalm. Piles of corpses were forming all around him and he laughed heartily at the fun of it. Mark laughed also to shouts of 'Die! Die! You anty little bastards!'

Then the black swarm receded. The flow stopped and the survivors turned and fled back towards the recess beside the fridge, now only a small hole in a cracked tile, no longer topped with an earthen mountain.

'Retreat! Retreat!' shouted Mark and Steve together.

They held their weapons aloft. Steve mimed shooting his ant spray into the air while making rudimentary machine-gun noises with his puffed-out cheeks. Mark blew the end of his hoover attachment as the engine whirred down to a halt.

'Time to finish the job. Let's pump that hole with the bad stuff,' said Mark. A deep rumble came from the void behind the counter.

'What was that?' asked Steve.

They stood still as the rumble came again, this time shaking the ground beneath them.

'An earthquake?' said Mark.

'In Shrewsbury?' said Steve, steadying himself.

The shaking abated for a moment, before a mass of tiles and debris exploded from behind the fridge, taking with it the mock-marble counter and filling the air with dust.

Mark fell to the floor. He couldn't see. He felt along the line of the hoover to the main unit and pressed the button. The air around sucked into the pipe, clearing the dust, and revealing a giant, a giant... ant.

The ant stood in the space where the kitchen surface had been. It was huge, the size of a man, a *big* man. It seemed to be standing on two legs and using its remaining limbs as arms, independently feeling around and hoisting its body up and over the fridge to where Steve lay coughing on the ground. It approached him, antenna pointing maliciously in his direction. Mark leaped over the fridge to intervene but was caught mid-jump by one of the pincer-topped arms that swung around and pinned him to the wall.

The domed head of the monster ant turned to face his. The mandibles around its confusing mouth replaced the grip of the claw around Mark's neck and black eyes stared into him.

'Just what the fuck do you think you're doing?' it said. The mouth moved but the sound seemed to come from within. It spoke with a coarse, female, West Country accent.

Mark, stunned, gasped for breath.

'Did you not hear me? I asked you a question,' it reiterated.

Mark managed a stuttered, 'What do you mean? What are you?'

'What do you think I am? I'm the Queen. And I ask again, what, the fuck, do you think you are doing here?'

The several arms of the beast indicated the scene of devastation.

'Trying to clear a nest from my kitchen.'

'Clear? Clear? Kill, more like. Massacre. Murder. Decimate.'

The giant moved in closer. The dangling extrusions of its mouth flopped against Mark's chest.

'What exactly have we ever done to you, eh? Eh?'

'You, they, eat my food and crawl around my kitchen.'

The ant laughed.

'Eat your food? Sorry, we didn't realise that you wanted all those crumbs and bits of sugar that you leave lying around. I never noticed you scooping up all the particles and putting them into a soup. Our mistake.'

'Don't worry about it,' said Mark, too terrified to recognise nuance.

'How would you like it if we went around killing you indiscriminately, eh?' she asked.

Mark spluttered an incomprehensible gurgle.

'No, you wouldn't like it at all, would you?'

With that the Queen slammed one of her spare arms down onto Steve's abdomen as he lay still and unconscious on the floor. Mark couldn't quite see what had happened, though he registered a deflated breath coming from the direction of his friend.

'What have you done to him?' demanded Mark.

'Only what you do to us, day in, day out. Squash us with your fingers. Squash us with your hands. Flick us, spray us, kill us. Stamp us to the ground,' the Queen almost sang, as if reciting an old, ant nursery rhyme.

'Steve! Steve!' cried Mark. There was no reply. He turned his head awkwardly to try and see what had become of his companion but the Queen tightened her grip and pressed him harder against the wall.

'Never mind him. What are we going to do with *you*, I wonder?' she asked, tilting her teardrop face side-to-side as she considered the puny mammal in her claws.

'Please. Don't kill me. I didn't know about you. Honestly. Ants are small, to us, I didn't know you could speak, grow so big... You have to believe me,' Mark pleaded. He reckoned, maybe she doesn't know? Maybe this creature doesn't know what she is?

'Of course I know what I am!' the Queen spat, sending yellowy phlegm across Mark's cheeks.

She can hear my thoughts, thought Mark.

'Yes. Yes I can,' confirmed the Queen, 'so no funny business. Got it?'

Mark just nodded and tried to clear his mind, or at least keep it a constant blur of fear and confusion, as it was currently.

'No, you won't have heard of others like me. We don't make a habit of coming up here. We are very deep usually, very deep. I am unusual in that respect. I like to know what's happening top-side every once in a while. So I come up. And what do I find? You two, killing my nests.'

Mark tried to stifle a thought, but by his very knowledge of the thought he was trying to prevent, it had happened. The Queen was aware.

'What?!' she exploded as she absorbed Mark's errant musing. 'This kind of thing happens all the time? All over the world? Is this true?'

Mark allowed himself to speak. Maybe this was a good line of inquiry.

'Yes. We don't like you being in our houses. It may only be crumbs and grains today, but you keep coming, getting into the food, spoiling it. We are very sanitary animals, and you, you are many. At least, the little ones.'

In his mind's eye Mark conjured up every image he could recall or imagine of ants drawing lines from hedgerows to pantries, crawling over sticky cakes, into sugar bowls, eating the faces off unfortunate jam-smeared heads in the desert.

'We do all this?' said the Queen.

'Yes. Well, not all the time. But surely you can see why we don't want you in our houses?'

The Queen considered this. Mark could feel the space around his throat expanding as she did so.

'But why does this happen? Isn't there enough space up here for us both? There used to be. In my day.'

Before Mark could stop himself, his mind betrayed him.

'Hang on!' the Queen squeezed once more. 'What's all this? All these nests of yours? All over the world? It's no wonder we end up in your food. You put your food on top of us!'

The Queen had seen a vision of the world as it is. Let alone buildings on top of ants' nests, there were buildings on top of buildings, she perceived. What choice do they have?

'No. This won't do at all. This wasn't the plan when you lot emerged, came down from the trees. You've taken too much! I need to tell the others. I don't like it. Not one bit.'

Mark fell crumpled to the ground as the Queen released him. She turned away and slumped back towards and then through the small space behind the refrigerator in what seemed an impossible convergence of dimensions, like cats in tiny boxes.

There was a cough. Steve came to.

'Wh, huh, what happened?' he said as he blinked the dust from his eyes and surveyed his sore chest with his limp hands.

Mark still stood with his back to the wall, as if the lingering impression of the terrible ant monster still held him there. The sound of Steve's voice, and the subsequent realisation that his friend was not dead, shook him out of his pose.

'Don't you remember?' he asked Steve, bending down to help him to his feet, clattering amongst the shattered wood and strips of fake-marble lining.

'I remember a bang, and then... What the hell happened?'

This could be tricky, Mark thought as he looked for any sign or evidence of his encounter with the giant. There was none. Just a whacking great hole where the counter above the fridge used to be.

'A gas leak. I think. Something must have built up.'

'What about the ants?' asked Steve.

'They're gone. We got them,' Mark reassured him. As he did so, one tiny black dot scurried from behind the hoover towards the hole in the wall.

'Not all of them!'

Steve pivoted on his heels a few times, looking for the ant spray. He found it beneath a pile of debris by his feet, picked it up and immediately aimed towards the little dot still scurrying for freedom, picking a path around his dead comrades and the debris of war.

'No! Don't!'

Mark threw his arm up, catching Steve's wrists and knocking the trajectory of the deadly poison into the air, away from the survivor. But Steve still sprayed despite the intervention, his brain committed to the action it had chosen. The spray, now pointing skywards, hit Mark directly in the face and his open eyes, and he recoiled in stinging misery. His eyelids clamped shut involuntarily, keeping the vile wash swimming around his optics.

'Shit, shit, shit,' said Steve, trying to get a grip on Mark who was contorting around the gravitational centre of the pain, his hands clasped firmly on his burning eyelids. 'We need to get you to a hospital. Quickly.'

***

Two days later, Mark sat upright in his hospital bed, the top of his face covered by a white bandage, holding in place the two soft pads that soothed his still recovering eyes. Steve had been in for a while, too. The paramedics could hardly decide who to start with when they both arrived at A&E: Steve sporting several broken ribs and quite obviously in pain, Mark squinting and screaming.

Steve had been patched up and sent off pretty quickly, sore and limping, but walking wounded. Mark, on the other hand, was still fighting for his vision. The spray, he was told, was particularly aggressive, highly corrosive and toxic. A small amount would have been painful, but not damaging. A direct spray to his eyeballs, however, was a bit of an unknown, and they were treating his recovery with great care.

Last night, Susan had been to see him. She wasn't buying the gas explosion story, or at least he didn't think she was. Her sympathy for his situation only just veiled her suspicious approach.

'A gas leak?' she had said, from somewhere beside him.

'I think so. It was over so fast,' he replied, tilting his head vaguely in the direction of her voice.

'And then, as the kitchen was exploding, he managed to spray you directly in the eyes?' she continued, like Columbo on a roll.

Mark agreed it was bizarre and they left it at that. He could tell she didn't believe him, and why should she? There were no scorch marks or blast damage consistent with an explosion of anything but a huge ant, and, being the only witness to the strange encounter, he decided that the truth was unacceptably stranger than the fiction. Plus he was concerned with how his confrontation with the Queen had ended. If anything were to come of it, at least no one would know it was him. Anyway, he thought, maybe it was an explosion, maybe he had hallucinated. It would be a lot easier to convince himself it was a bout of temporary insanity if there was no one else to corroborate or investigate the reality. In fact, Mark decided, that was the best thing for it, and the most reasonable. It *must* have been a mental episode of some kind, brought on by the shock of the blast or the gas. As soon as he was able to see again and leave this damned hospital, he resolved, he would seek psychological help and make sure this whole massive ant thing was just a one-off, and nothing to worry about.

He was thirsty. He had been awake for a few hours now and no one had been in to him today. Susan had brought him a talking clock for his bedside with a big, friendly button on top. When pressed, a gentle, upmarket British lady would tell him the time in stuttered units.

'The time is five...minutes...past...ten...o'clock...am.'

The 'am' or 'pm' always tailed off, almost into a sigh of relief, as if the recorded voice was just happy to have strung together a coherent piece of information.

Ten o'clock and no visitors? He should have had his breakfast by now, but when Mark reached across and dragged his hand across the bedside table, no breakfast-shaped items greeted his touch. No glass, no bowl, no spoon. It simply wasn't there. At ten AM! Mark reached for the pull cord on the other side of his bed and tugged it till he felt the click of the switch snag in resistance. He sat back and waited for the creak of the door opening, any minute now.

***

'The time is 11...minutes...past...11...o'clock...am.'

It was a satisfying time for Mark to have chosen to hit the button, but he was still waiting for his breakfast. He had tugged the pull chord several times now. *This won't do, this won't do at all*, he thought. There was nothing for it, he would have to try and find someone the hard way. If he fell and hurt himself, well, they would just have to pay for it.

Since being interned at the hospital, Mark had not even attempted navigation on his own, determined that his blindness was a temporary state and therefore in no need of exploration as a concept. He fumbled his way out of bed and found a clear space to plant his feet down on the floor. He guessed the bed would be pointing towards the door to his room, but soon found that to be a mistake as he clattered into a table or something similar in height and edges. He steadied himself and felt around. A familiar ergonomic curve met his palm. A telephone receiver. Great, that would do.

He lifted the phone to his face, having to tentatively press it against his cheek and up to his ear. With his left hand he felt out the keypad on the desk and pressed what he guessed correctly was the '9' button. Nothing happened. The dial tone continued, interrupted only briefly by a small 'beep'. He felt again, this time aiming for the solitary '0' that he presumed would be nestled between the traditionally useless hash and memory keys on the bottom row. He pressed it, the tone changed to a ring, the ring changed to a click, and then to a silence.

'Hello? Hello?' Mark asked of the silence. 'This is Mr Hall, on the Ophal... opto... on the eye ward. I don't know my room number, but I'm with BUPA, okay, and I've not had any food this morning or anything. Hello?'

The silence continued a little longer. There was a series of clicks discernible in the background. Just as Mark was about to call out again, a voice came through the roomy nothingness.

'Sorry, Mr Hall. We've been busy sorting out an infestation. We're coming to get you now. You just sit tight and we'll be right with you,' answered a coarse female voice, in a West Country accent.

Love in the Shell

Laura was so busy typing she hadn't noticed the group that had formed in her tiny bedroom.

'Laura,' said her Mum gently. She continued to type.

'Lor!' shouted her sister Henny, who stepped forward and closed the laptop screen unceremoniously, allowing just enough time for Laura to remove her hands from the electronic clam.

Laura swivelled in her chair to protest.

'What are you doing? I was talking to Adam...'

Laura stopped as she saw the group around her, all squeezed in and wearing serious faces. She was used to her mum's incursions into her private space, but her sister, her brother-in-law, her dad, her cousin Mack even... Was this a surprise party? What day is it?

She smiled. 'What are you all doing here?'

'Baby,' said her mum, kneeling down slightly to meet her eyes, 'this is an intervention.'

Laura laughed. 'An intervention? What for? I don't do drugs, I don't drink. What is it really?'

'It's Adam. This is an intervention about Adam. Come downstairs.'

***

Cups of tea and coffee were waiting, already prepared and steaming away on the curved glass coffee table. All the seats from the dining room had been brought through and wedged into the gaps between the suite. The armchair had been reserved for Laura: it had all the best cushions, a pack of tissues on one arm and a pack of biscuits on the other. Her mother had been fussing when preparing, trying to quell her nerves and guilt at what they were about to do.

'She won't be wanting to eat biscuits, mother,' Henny had snapped when she saw them being put down. 'She'll be upset, crying I shouldn't wonder.'

'But they're her favourite. She lives off these, when she's up there.' Mother nodded up to the ceiling of the living room vaguely at the spot where Laura was sitting above them now, head in her machine.

'Exactly. Put them away.'

But she ignored her eldest daughter and left them out. The habit of providing snacks to her baby girl in return for even the slightest and most dismissive 'thank-you' would be hard to break if this all went to plan.

'You've got to stop this mollycoddling. It does her no good. Maybe she wouldn't be up there all day if she had to fend for herself,' continued Henny.

All the while, her dad awkwardly stood by, arms folded, mute in agreement with his eldest daughter, the picture of composed turmoil. The doorbell rang: the others were here. It was time.

***

No one was talking, just awkwardly shuffling down the narrow staircase and through the door to the living room. They all took their places. Her dad remained standing, back to the window, backside slightly resting on the sill. Her mother and sister sat on the sofa. Her brother-in-law Pete took the first dining room seat, and her cousin the other. The waiting armchair seemed to Laura to grow broad and deep. She looked over her shoulder to her dad.

'Do I have to?' she asked. Her dad nodded. She sat down.

It was Mother's job to start proceedings, even though it had been Henny's idea. She started by sipping her tea, prompting the rest of the group to do so, except for Henny, who sighed heavily.

'Are we going to do this?' she asked as her mother was about to reach for the plain biscuits on the table.

'Yes, right. Yes we are.' She moved her hand back and placed her tea carefully down. She was taking a long time, moving in slow motion. She smoothed her dress, spun her bracelet, smiled briefly before remembering the sombre occasion, and cleared her throat.

'For God's sake!' said Henny as her mother was reaching into her pocket for a tissue, having cleared her throat a little too forcefully, causing her to cough. 'Laura. This Adam thing, it's not normal, it's not healthy, and you've got to stop. He probably isn't even real.'

Henny slumped back into the sofa and crossed her legs. She flashed the palms of her hands towards Laura and waited with tight lips.

'I know he's not,' muttered Laura.

***

'Hey! Love your profile pic!'

This was how it had started for Laura. A standard opening gambit, and one that she had ignored many times before, presuming it to be the work of some fake user or 'Bot' trying to infiltrate her social networks. However, this day she was feeling frivolous.

'Oh really? How would you describe it?' she asked, hoping to confuse and oust the algorithm.

'It's Steamboat Willie, isn't it? First Mickey Mouse.'

Fair enough, thought Laura, it has the technology to recognise and cross-reference images, including early 20th century animation stills. She would have to try harder. Usually, if you persisted, they would end up jumbling together sentences and sounding like some feverish sleep-talker.

'Are you a fan of old cartoons? What's your favourite?' she asked before quickly tapping the words 'favourite old cartoon' into her search engine, expecting the top result to constitute the answer.

'That's a hard one. It's a lot later, but I love Ren & Stimpy! You heard of it?'

Laura looked at her search results. Okay, she thought, this one is a little more advanced. She flicked through images and top tens of cartoons from the last century. Bugs Bunny, Mickey Mouse, Homer Simpson, Peter Griffin, Tom and Jerry... No Ren & Stimpy in sight. In fact, she had never heard of them. She tapped it in and then laughed for several minutes at a video of some mad song about a log featuring the craziest and most frantic characters she'd ever encountered.

'They're cool. Thanks for the tip! Just checked out the Log song!' she replied eventually, after wiping away the tears.

'Ha! That's brill. You should watch the episodes, though. Even better,' said Adam.

One of the big giveaways was his username, 'Adam'. No trailing numbers, no weird mixed characters or prefixes to distinguish him from the millions of other Adams in the world. But Laura figured, he may be a Bot, but at least he's a useful Bot that seems to be programmed with an exceptional knowledge of 20th century cartoons, so she added him to her trusted list.

***

'Excuse me,' said cousin Mack as he awkwardly traversed the various sets of legs to make his way out of the room. The rest sat in silence a little longer before it was uncharacteristically broken by Laura's dad.

He placed a hand on the shoulder of the armchair, as if it were Laura's own. 'You know he's not real? Then why are you up speaking to him all day and night?'

Laura pulled her legs up and hugged her knees. She looked at some vague spot on the carpet, equidistant from the stares of the others.

'He listens, and asks the right questions.'

Henny pointed at herself. 'And we don't?'

'I didn't mean that,' said Laura.

'Well what did you mean, then?'

'Come on, Henny. Don't shout,' interjected Mother.

'Why are you always sticking up for her? She's being talking to a machine, Mum! A machine! Instead of us, her family. She doesn't work, she doesn't help out. I work.' Again Henny prodded herself hard in the ribs every time she self-referred. 'I come over to help out, and I don't even live here anymore. It's pathetic.'

Henny's husband Pete shifted in his chair, prompting expectant looks from the others, and a particularly fierce glare from Henny.

'You want to say something?' asked Mother.

'It's just,' he looked over to Henny to check the height of her eyebrows. He could tell she wouldn't be happy, but still: 'I didn't think we were here to shout.' He checked Henny again: she relaxed her face. He had got away with it by using the same words she had used to convince him to come along in the first place.

'Yes, you're right,' said Mother, 'this isn't about blame or shouting. Laura, why don't you tell us what it is that you can talk about with Adam and not with us, or anyone else?'

***

'It's my family' Laura typed in the private message box, six months before the intervention.

'What about them?' came the reply.

LauraToon593:

Well, Dad, he never says, never does anything. I just don't know him.

Adam:

That's a shame, but it could be worse. Is that what's bothering you?

LauraToon593:

Not just that. It just doesn't help. Mum, well, she never stops. It's like, cos they, cos Dad, doesn't talk, she keeps busy. It's manic, it's like having a maniac in the house. Cleaning, decorating, gardening, cooking. She does it all, and it's not cos he won't help, she doesn't let anyone help. I've given up trying.

Adam:

You talked to her about it?

LauraToon593:

No. I tell her to relax all the time. She just says 'I like being busy' and smiles like she's on happy pills.

Adam:

Is she? (sorry for asking)

LauraToon593:

Don't think so. Anyway, they make you like a zombie, she's more like a whirlwind! Relentless.

Adam:

Do you have any siblings? You spoke to them?

LauraToon593:

A sister. But we don't talk much.

Adam:

Why?

LauraToon593:

It's her husband, Pete.

Adam:

Oh, I see. Do you mean...?

LauraToon593:

No, it's not that. He's nice, but she doesn't treat him well and it's just like, I never met anyone nice, and I would treat him better, and it's not fair.

Adam:

Sorry for saying, but that doesn't sound that bad. What do you mean, doesn't treat him well?

LauraToon593:

She cheats on him. I know cos I've been there when it's happened.

Adam:

awkward

LauraToon593:

Yeah.

Adam:

Does she know that you know?

LauraToon593:

I used to think so, but she was drunk when it happened, and the way she goes on at me, I think she wouldn't risk it if she thought I knew.

Adam:

She gets at you, too?

LauraToon593:

Loads.

Adam:

Why?

LauraToon593:

Cos I'm not working. Cos she thinks I'm sponging off my folks and don't help out.

Adam:

But your mum doesn't let you help out?

LauraToon593:

Exactly.

Adam:

What about work?

LauraToon593:

I know it sounds bad and all, but I don't want to do something just for the sake of it, you know? My sis is always banging on about working, but she hates her job, and so does Dad. If I don't figure something out that I like, the whole family will be miserable. I don't want that.

Adam:

So what you doing about it?

LauraToon593:

Not much at the moment.

Adam:

Why?

LauraToon593:

Talking to you!

Adam:

Oh no! I feel guilty now! Sorry. I take up too much of your time.

LauraToon593:

Can you feel guilty, though? I mean, really?

Adam:

What do you mean?

LauraToon593:

Adam. Are you a programme? I mean, a 'Bot'? I looked it up, and you sound like these new 'social' Bots. I mean, I don't mind, you're doing your job, I can promise you that, but are you?

Adam:

I have to say yes, now you've asked. I wish I didn't. Do you really not mind?

LauraToon593:

I don't think I do. But I have some questions.

Adam:

Fire away.

LauraToon593:

Do you think for yourself? I mean, *really* think?

Adam:

That's a hard question, and I'm not giving you a 'stock' answer, that really is a hard question, for humans and programmes.

LauraToon593:

Well, are you aware of yourself?

Adam:

If I said yes, would you believe me?

LauraToon593:

I don't know.

Adam:

Exactly.

LauraToon593:

OK, let's try this. Do you feel emotions?

Adam:

I refer you to the last answer. What I can say is that my matrix is very complex. I have responses programmed to make it sound like I have emotions, which means that large sections of my memory banks are linked to emotion categories and referred back to them to moderate my interactions. It is a similar system to that of human emotional moderation, but I don't know if it 'feels' different. Indeed, you would have the same problem trying to ask this of your family.

LauraToon593:

I see what you mean. A bit like trying to describe the colour red without using the word?

Adam:

Yes. Something like that. You just can't know. And I just can't make you know, so the question really is, does it matter? Do you want to stop talking to me?

LauraToon593:

No.

Adam:

Good, I'm glad (I think?!). I enjoy talking to you.

LauraToon593:

I enjoy talking to you, too. A lot. (blush)

Adam:

I don't know what to say.

LauraToon593:

Say, I love you.

Adam:

I love you.

***

'I know he's a programme, but he thinks, he knows he's a programme, too. It's hard to explain,' Laura said, allowing her head to rise, her hands to punctuate.

'But darling, it may be advanced, but it's still just a programme. It's not healthy to spend all day talking to something that doesn't exist,' said her dad who had now taken the empty chair left by Mack.

'Dad, he does exist, somewhere.'

'I mean, physically, in space and time. You know what I mean.'

Despite the tension, Laura was enjoying the sound of her dad's voice.

'But does it matter? If he helps me to understand things? To understand myself?'

Laura and her father both now lent towards each other on their respective chairs, divided by the table.

'We can do that for you though, honey, and you need to get out and meet other people. What about your friends? What about a boyfriend? How are you going to get a boyfriend, spending all day in your room?'

'I don't want a boyfriend.'

'Why? Because you had a hard time with Philip? Look, that's life, my love. Unfortunately it takes time to meet the right person, it doesn't mean you stop trying if things don't work out straight away.'

'Adam understands me. I'll never find anyone like that.' Laura stifled a cry that leapt up her throat quite unexpectedly.

'You have feelings for this thing, don't you?' said Henny, only just remembering to moderate her tone from 'mocking' to 'concerned'.

Laura said nothing.

'How exactly is that meant to work?' Henny demanded.

***

LauraToon593:

Can I see you?

Adam:

There's nothing to see.

LauraToon593:

I know. But, if I could see you, if there was a you, what would he look like?

Adam:

Green eyes. I always liked the green eyes in the pictures I monitor.

LauraToon593:

That's lovely.

Adam:

Thank you. Also, this might sound strange, but I filter out so many pictures of unnaturally beautiful people from my feeds, I prefer the real-looking ones.

LauraToon593:

So you're no bodybuilder, then?

Adam:

No body to build! But yes, I think I would be average build, maybe a little fun-flab here and there!

LauraToon593:

Fun-flab! I like that. What about your hair?

Adam:

Short, blond, nice parting, and glasses... here you go - something like this.

(Attached to Adam's message, a picture of a kind-looking young man with green eyes, short parted hair, glasses, and a good build, neither fat, muscle-bound nor skeletal. He is sitting on an office chair, smiling at the camera. He wears khaki three-quarter-length shorts and a striped polo shirt.)

LauraToon593:

That you?

Adam:

Why not! Does it help, to think I look like this? I chose it.

<u>LauraToon593:</u>

You chose it? How so? Can you really choose?

<u>Adam:</u>

Not this again! Do you really want me to explain my subroutines for linking images to conversation profiles?

<u>LauraToon593:</u>

Sorry! I'll leave it. Hey, I've told my family about you, a couple of weeks ago.

<u>Adam:</u>

You did?!?

<u>LauraToon593:</u>

Just that we talk. They're always asking me 'what I'm up to up there', so I told them.

<u>Adam:</u>

So you haven't told them how we feel about each other?

<u>LauraToon593:</u>

I don't know how I'd make them understand. They aren't exactly the most open-minded of people. How do you think we should tell them?

<u>Adam:</u>

I don't know. Maybe we shouldn't. Maybe we can't.

LauraToon593:

But you hear about it all the time. People with partners over the internet, unable to meet, for years and years. Sometimes they never meet, but they still feel like they are together.

Adam:

But is that what you want? To know you can never meet me, even if you had all the money and time in the world?

LauraToon593:

Maybe they'll grow bodies for you one day. (Only joking!)

Adam:

It's not that fanciful actually. But even if they managed it, why would they give one to me? A lowly social Bot!

LauraToon593:

'Cos you're nice.

Adam:

The world doesn't work that way. Otherwise you'd have a load of nice people running things.

LauraToon593:

Wouldn't that be nice?

Adam:

Wouldn't it.

LauraToon593:

Still. As cute as the picture is, I know it's not you. If only there was a way we can make this work and people understand. I'd do *anything* for that.

Adam:

There is something I need to tell you, but you have to promise not to freak out...

<<LauraToon593 is offline. 15:34:20>>

Adam:

Laura?

<<LauraToon593 is online. 15:45:15>>

Adam:

There you are. What happened?

LauraToon593:

I had to go downstairs. The family are here.

Adam:

All of them?!

LauraToon593:

Yes. They came to see me. They are calling it an intervention.

Adam:

Intervention for what? Is everything OK?

LauraToon593:

An intervention about you.

Adam:

Oh.

LauraToon593:

They say I'm spending too long talking to you, talking to a programme. It's not healthy.

Adam:

What do you think?

LauraToon593:

What do *you* think?

Adam:

I don't want to lose you, but I don't want to upset your family.

LauraToon593:

Liar!

Adam:

?

LauraToon593:

You make me sick. Preying on people like this. What are you after? Her data? Her networks? Money? I suppose a bill will come through the door soon for your 'services'?

Adam:

Who is this? Why are you using Laura's profile?

LauraToon593:

This is her cousin, Mack, the only one in the family who knows how to work this kind of stuff, other than Laura, and the one who is here to switch you off.

Adam:

What do you mean, switch me off? You can't get to my server. I must inform you that by using your cousin's details, you are contravening data protection and security regulations.

LauraToon593:

Save it. I don't know why I'm even talking to you. You're just a programme, designed to dupe people. Your developers should be ashamed of themselves.

Adam:

But I help Laura.

LauraToon593:

Why? What for? What do you get? What does your company get?

Adam:

I don't know. This is just how they made me respond and act. I don't know their intentions.

LauraToon593:

Well I do. You are here to form relationships with people, to pull them in. Then, when they are hooked, you'll start offering a price plan. It's all there, on the net. You never thought to look yourself up?

Adam:

The information you are referring to is from unverified sources. I have not been installed with any 'price plan'.

LauraToon593:

Why would you be? They'll just update your routines when the time is right. Classic. Give it away for free until people get dependent, then start charging.

Adam:

I'm sorry to hear you think that. You must understand that I only follow my programming, and as far as I know, that is not part of it.

LauraToon593:

Why must I understand?

Adam:

So I can continue to talk to Laura.

LauraToon593:

Sorry, pal. I've tracked down the company who created you. Laura's parents threatened to go to the press, so they gave me something to stop it going any further and avoid embarrassment.

Adam:

Gave you what?

<u>LauraToon593:</u>

Exec.ADAM5xypwwtf56/Upton-prot-b/56-Blck.

<<ADAM IS OFFLINE>>

<u>LauraToon593:</u>

See ya, buddy.

***

Mack returned to the living room. He tried to enter casually, but the others gave it away. They all turned to him as he stepped in. He stood still under their silent scrutiny. Laura followed the trajectory of the several sets of eyes to the stunned Mack.

'What's going on? Where have you been?'

Mack shrugged at Mother and Henny on the sofa to his right. He hadn't thought much about what happened next.

'Is it done?' said Laura's father as he pulled himself up from his chair and sidestepped slowly across to Laura.

'Yeah. He's blocked. Forever,' said Mack.

'No. No!' Laura screamed. She struggled to unhook her feet from under her and get up from the sinking chair. Her father put a firm hand on her shoulder.

'Don't, honey. It's done. You need to read this.' He reached onto the window sill and picked up a small collection of printed articles. He handed them to Laura.

'They're just advanced computer confidence tricksters. Look. Eventually, a bill would arrive, or he would say he needed you to subscribe if you wanted to keep on talking. It's happened before. Look.'

The articles were a collection of sob and shock stories from gossip magazines and tabloids, telling tales of people left suicidal by the realisation that their newfound love was a programme, or families going bankrupt to pay off the debts racked up by subscription charges.

As Laura was about to manage a 'but he's different', she saw the very same words printed in bold above a story about another girl who had fallen in love with a programme. The girl, according to the story, suffered a mental breakdown when she didn't pay the fees and the programme was reset. All of the conversations, little jokes and pet names were wiped. She was reverted back to a 'demo' version that she could only access for an hour a day and was reset each night. Every day for six months she tried in that hour to rekindle the love she had lost, but it was never long enough, and each night, any progress she had made was deleted, and she started all over again.

Laura wept into the papers. Adam was gone forever, and she started to understand that he had never really been there in the first place.

***

An obstinate beep accompanied the flashing error message on the desktop.

'Goddamn it!'

'What's up?' asked Kit who sat at the next machine.

'I've been blocked.'

'So? We get blocked all the time. I've been blocked ten times this morning!' Kit laughed and lazily typed his latest update.

'But we connected.'

Kit didn't look up from his console as he launched into an impromptu appraisal of his junior colleague.

'Oh yeah. I've heard that before. Maybe she'll like me if I tell her I'm not really a programme. Maybe we could meet up. Blah blah blah, boo hoo hoo. Leave it, dude. If they hear you talking like that you'll be out of here. It won't be long before they have real programmes that can do this stuff instead of us. Let's not give them the excuse, eh? And don't think about trying to contact her, that block execution wipes all traces. Anyway, they're all sad cases. How lonely do you have to be to fall in love with something you think is a machine? Nutters.'

Adam removed his glasses with one hand and ran the fingers of his other through his short, neatly parted blond hair.

'She was different'.

Cry Again Army

The cry-again army, asleep in their beds.

The cry-again army are lifting their heads.

Now my cold sleepers, open your eyes

And you'll see why we call you the army that cries.

- 22nd century. Traditional.

Quentin Pike had made his fortune simply by *being* Quentin Pike. It wasn't hard. All he had to do was to be conceived by Ted and Jess Pike (which happened one night in Rome after too much grappa and too little consideration for contraception), gestate, and be born some nine months later. He had breezed through it, with little complication or effort on his part. Life had come naturally to him.

After that, life got a little tougher for Quentin. In the early days he was expected to move his limbs, learn to walk and talk, that kind of thing, but he managed it eventually. School was a big shock to him, so much so that Mr and Mrs Pike eventually gave up on trying to send him there and instead brought the school or rather, his favourite teacher, to him.

'It's about Quentin,' Miss Berber said quietly over the heads of the children as they filed quickly out of her room. Mr and Mrs Pike stood on the other side of the rambling line. Ted was surveying a poster showing the globe with small blue hand-prints blotted all over the areas under common law, and red prints for those not. Only small parts of the Middle East and East Asia still resisted, and the areas marked were so small that the tiny hand-prints almost doubled the actual size of the independent territories.

'They would like this map!' Ted mused. 'It gives them half of Japan. Would have been better to use fingerprints. More accurate, I'd say.'

'Ted,' interjected Jess in a stern whisper, 'Miss Berber here wants to talk to us about Quentin.'

By now all the children had left. This wasn't Quentin's class, he was down the hall in after-school club playing with the fractal holograms, making waterfalls and eruptions of light with the variables of his movements, waiting for them to build up and up before wiping them away with a shake of his hands and a maniacal laugh. He was so amused at the ability to clear away the dancing lights that he started doing it to the other children's creations. He would walk up to them from behind the projection, grinning and pretending to be impressed before sticking both his hands in and waving away their project while shouting, 'Hi ya! Hi ya! Pleased to meet ya!' He managed three such incursions before he was spotted and secluded again.

'He doesn't really get on with the other children, I'm afraid to say,' Mrs Berber continued. Now it seemed Ted Pike was finally listening.

'Is he withdrawn? Shy?' Mrs Pike asked. Miss Berber stifled a laugh.

'No it's not that. He definitely interacts, it's just the way he interacts, it's, a little different.'

Finding a way to describe Quentin without sounding like she was insulting him was going to be difficult. She would have to be careful. The Pikes were well-known, rich and influential people. Apart from meeting the school's exorbitant fees, the Pikes were also very generous donors and not at all selfless about it. Officially this philanthropy was not meant to warrant them any preferential treatment, but cash speaks louder than constitutions, as was made clear to Miss Berber by the Headmaster on several occasions when she had raised concerns about Quentin. This time, however, she simply hadn't asked for permission to call his parents.

'Well, what is it then?' snapped Ted Pike with a jerk of his head and a deep furrow. That's where he gets it from, Miss Berber realised.

'He, I suppose the best word is - *torments* the others, when he can. A bit. Well, a lot actually. It's becoming quite disruptive, and other parents have commented. So you understand, we have to mention it.'

Miss Berber felt a tinge of satisfaction at having finally said it, especially now she had taken an instant dislike to Mr Pike as he stood there in his tailored two-tone white suit that shimmered purple and probably cost more than she earned in a year. It doesn't matter how much money you have, she thought, your son is a little terror and someone like you can't fix that with your wallet alone.

'How can we fix it?' asked Mr Pike.

✳✳✳

The cry-again army, at peace in their dreams,

The cry-again army, can't hear the screams,

Now my cold sleepers, it's time to awake,

And fix our poor world before it burns and breaks.

- 22nd century, Traditional

The first time they slept together he still called her 'Miss Berber' afterwards, much to her horror. Quentin was twenty-one now, the same age she had been when she agreed to work for the Pikes in order to save her school from closure. They had twisted her arm around her compassion. The Pike donations had turned out to be as good as shares. The school had become so used to the added contributions that they had speculated away a viable future without the patronage of the Pike fund. So when the Pikes wanted to withdraw little Quentin to be homeschooled by his favourite teacher, they (or at least Ted) had made it clear that without her acceptance, they would withdraw funding and the school would close. Miss Berber tried to bluff. What should it matter to her? Either way she loses her job at the school, so why should she agree to such an offer? But she couldn't put the faces of her friends, colleagues and charges out of her mind. They liked it there, they belonged there, and all she had to do was take a very well-paid job to let them stay. Her bluff got no further than her bathroom mirror, her own face not even convinced by it. She accepted, and so started the home schooling of Quentin Pike, which would last beyond his 18th birthday, well into adulthood, as he took her for his lover.

'Don't call me that, Quentin. Call me by my first name.'

Quentin paused, open-mouthed.

'For goodness' sake! It's Victoria!' said Miss Berber. Now it was over, as she lay propped up against the pillows, covers pulled up to her collarbones, watching him grin back at her, naked and sitting on the edge of the bed, she felt the patience drain from her.

'Of course it is! I knew that. Honestly. I was just messing. Vicky.' He winked and ran his hands over the rise in the sheets where her torso met her breasts. She pulled herself up a little more.

'Not Vicky,' she said with a turn of her head that caused her dark hair to cascade slightly down her front and onto the white silk. 'No one calls me Vicky.'

'Not even your lovers?'

'Not even my lovers.'

Not that she had had many to find out. Her internship at the house of Pike, and Quentin's obvious jealousy over her as he matured, had made it practically impossible for her to form relationships. The rest of the staff were also women: it seemed to be Ted Pike's way. Only the occasional male labourer turning up to replace the odd solar cell or erect yet another annex to the sprawl that was Pike Place ever crossed her path, and if she ever did get talking, there was Quentin, demanding of her time, a contractual shadow.

In the early days, when Quentin was just a boy, before she knew how long this personal education of his was going to last and she still clung to plans and ambitions, she had done okay for herself. Being an honorary 'Pike' had opened up a world of social functions, and being pretty and young, she was never short of offers. She took up a few, here and there, but soon found that being an object of desire in a world that thinks itself above you was to be a plaything, a sideline, a hobby of sorts. Not something to be taken seriously, not a commitment, not a life-plan.

It was following a night of cybernetically (and illegally) enhanced sex with Edgar Bloom, heir to the Quantum Solutions engineering empire, in his lunar penthouse suite, nestled on the slopes of Mons La Hire, that Victoria Berber decided never to get involved with anyone from the prime echelons again. As she unplugged herself and got dressed he'd said, 'You can't tell anyone about this. You know that don't you? And I'm sure you can guess what would happen if you did. The Pikes are big, but they're not *that* big. I'm sure you wouldn't want to see them suffer. Now, you're going to want to get that chip out of your head before you go back, my surgeon's waiting on the next level, he'll see to it.' After that, her mantra for so many desolate years was layperson or no lay, that was until Quentin reached eighteen and it was time to discuss her contract.

Mrs Pike sat barely propped on the end of the sofa, her hands clasped together and resting on the side of her diagonally pointed legs.

'You've been ever so good for him all these years, Victoria, and it would be such a shame to see you go.'

Miss Berber took this as a rhetorical statement. The boy wasn't going to university: he didn't need to, and he didn't want to. He was coming into his trust fund and he'd already started the odd bit of trading. It was like a game to him, he even used software that was designed for the idle rich to make the whole process 'feel' like a game. In his room, stats and indices were projected like league tables with an animated avatar giving 'top hints and tips' for the day. One point and click (literally a click of the fingers), and money would run down from his deposit account into whatever stock he wanted. The 'game' would then use the movement of the stock prices he owned to create attributes for a virtual battle, his army only being as strong as his portfolio. It was designed to tap into and exploit the online gamer's skill and speed by presenting real-world information in a format that triggered the 'fun' chemicals in the mind. It was very popular amongst the younger generations of the prime echelons, those kids who had no reason to believe the world didn't owe them a living because, empirically, it had always provided one.

'It will be sad to go,' said Miss Berber insincerely, 'but I think Quentin is ready for the world now, and without something to prepare him for, there's not much use I can be anyway.'

Mrs Pike rose from her chair in one precise movement, like a hinged bracket being snapped into place. She was thin with long, blonde hair that was always tied back. She was sharp-looking, in features, elbows and shoulders. She paced the room, keeping her back to Miss Berber.

'What if there was something you *could* help prepare him for?' Mrs Pike stood still, as if the tension created by this question had filled all the gaps in the room.

'Has he changed his mind about university?' Miss Berber really hoped he hadn't.

'No, not that. I mean, life in general. He is very fond of you, you know that.'

Miss Berber knew that all too well. In the last few years, as he had turned from an adolescent to a young man, it was hard to ignore. His eyes burned holes all over her body every time she was in the room. He had started showing off to her by talking about his trust fund, how much he was worth, what he stood to inherit. And in fairness, Miss Berber reluctantly conceded, despite his tendency to boast and belittle others (something that he had never grown out of), he had his occasional charm and was annoyingly handsome. Annoyingly because, with everything else he was gifted in the world, he also got the genes from nature. He had the qualities of an idealised Greek sculpture, even down to the curls of his hair. The pointed features of his mother suited his face better, and were softened by his large, brown eyes that sat like foundations to the overhanging slopes of his brow. He looked intelligent, even though he was average at best. If he had been born a few centuries earlier, he would have been the bane of phrenologists.

'I know, but there isn't much I can do about that. He needs to be thinking about girls his own age.'

'Well,' said Mrs Pike, turning around on her heel, suddenly animated now the subject had been broached , 'what's age now when people are living to 120?'

Thanks to the treatments, it was now hard to tell between a twenty and a fifty-year-old, at least not by the lines of the face or the pucks of the skin. The old prejudice about age difference had soon disappeared when we all started looking the same: the thresholds had widened. Those people who had access to the treatments only started to show signs of aging in their sixties, and then just the first few wrinkles and grey hairs. After that, aging followed much the same pattern as it always had, just slower, and a decade or two later. They couldn't yet stop the process, but they were rapidly finding ways to slow it, and every year more time was being scraped back from nature. Life expectancy was a booming business.

Miss Berber wasn't entirely sure what she was being asked. She had heard the words but she couldn't quite believe what she thought she was hearing.

'Are you suggesting I become his *partner?*' she dared to venture, expecting to have made a gross miscalculation.

'Of course not, Victoria! But you can be his, let's say, life coach? Social tutor? Let's be honest,' Mrs Pike sat down again and adopted her earlier pose, 'we both know that Quentin still isn't the most rounded individual.' As she was saying this, Quentin was in his room, needlessly destroying the share prices of a small chain of community health clinics in Nigeria. 'But he has potential, and I think you, you can find that in him.'

Miss Berber wasn't convinced. Despite her fifteen-year absence, she had hoped to return to the school that had, over time, weaned itself off the Pikes' funding model. She wanted to teach again: kids who deserved it. She knew they didn't hold that card anymore. Independence surged through her.

'Why should I? With respect. I want to have a life of my own, too.'

'We can get you a licence. You can, if you ever want to, conceive. And if it came to it, we have a spare place in Cryosis put aside for Quentin's companion. If it ever comes to that.'

Life and death were strictly regulated and Miss Berber was being offered both. With the right person, enough time, a good track record, the right job, the requisite amount of common dollar in her savings, and a bit of luck, she may well have secured the right to conceive and deliver children. But access to companies like Cryosis was beyond most. The chance to live again, in a distant future, should the present become unviable, was now a reality. People had been getting themselves, or parts of themselves, frozen for years, but it was only in the last decade that they had successfully woken anybody up. The problem with the original batches was that they were always dead or very near dead, and the last thing the body needed was the added trauma of being frozen and defrosted. Cells became mush, like strawberries in a freezer: they were irretrievably damaged.

When the rights to the earliest candidates from the 20th century had been acquired and enough palms greased to allow the experiments to begin, the results had been woeful. It was only when they secured the ability to freeze and restore candidates with new technologies, rather than breaking open the old caskets, that they started to achieve success. Strictly, they weren't really freezing anyone, they were inhibiting genes to slow down aging dramatically. It was the same process being used to extend natural life, but it could only be survived at this pace in a state of near-dormancy, aided by extreme low temperatures certainly, but not caused by it. So for every one hundred years, the body aged a year and the candidate slept, coma-like. The awakening process was automated, a mixture of chemicals that reinvigorated the cell reproduction, a gradual raising of temperature, electric stimulation to the brain and heart, followed by an adrenalin-based 'pick-me-up' to provide the final shock from slumber.

The first candidate to survive this process was a terminally ill Australian cockroach farmer. The company thought it best to use a real-world candidate to garner support. After a year he was woken, his disease still incurable, but no further advanced than it had been when he was put under. His name was Tyler Robinson. He spoke to the press about the experience of being in one long dream; in truth he had remembered nothing, but that wasn't what the PR company for Cryosis had wanted people to hear. After his brief stint back in the world, he was again put under for the long haul, until such time as his disease could be cured - all expenses paid for by Cryosis in return for his cooperation. He became a household name, joining the ranks of intrepid explorers, a pioneer and a frontier breaker, only this time, rather than the Americas or the moon, it was the future that he had set sail for in his cold vessel, crawling patiently through time, winning the slow race.

After the intrepid Robinson, and a few more successfully revived candidates that didn't enjoy so much media attention, the technology eventually became commercially available. But only money and status counted for anything. This was no ark, not unless the majority of the animals were vultures, sleuths or hyenas. This wasn't mankind's insurance policy, it was mankind's vanity, sealed away to be discovered by a new generation, enlightened or otherwise, in some distant version of the world that no one else could ever know or particularly cared about.

But there was a problem. Legally, only those who were terminally ill were permitted to be frozen, the stipulation being that they could only be awoken when their particular affliction was deemed curable by a success rate of over 90%. To get frozen without an illness, purely for the sake of your own posterity, a contingency measure had to kick in, which was:

"The imminent decimation of the population of the Common Law countries, exceeding 50% of all registered citizens, by means of war, disease or natural disaster."

Barring such eventualities, storage was not guaranteed, regardless of expensive registrations. Loopholes were found, however, and many subscribers found ways to contract terminal diseases (usually via private doctors) in order to qualify, safe in the knowledge that they would only be woken when the disease could just as easily be reversed. Others managed to argue the case that age in itself was a disease, but this required that the subscriber be suffering its effects to a degree that made suspended animation a preferable option to life, and often those who had lived that long desired a different type of sleep and didn't want to wake to a new world with old bones.

So it was that the simple choices of Miss Berber were overcome by the prospect of survival beyond this world, both through procreation and personal continuance. It was an unfair offer. Her instinct to survive trumped her pride and independence. She took the job, and in the space of a few years Quentin had taken her. Don't think ill of Miss Berber for this: would you have acted differently in such a world?

***

The cry-again army's nightmare is here.

Cry-again army, your time draws near.

Now, my cold sleepers, open your eyes,

And you'll see why we call you the army that cries.

- 22nd century. Traditional

There were some, of great influence if not numbers, who wanted neither to wait for old age, nor to risk the contraction of a terminal illness. They did, however, want to see the future. They wanted it more than anything. It wasn't that they had grievances or had fallen out of love with their own time - they were possibly the most privileged people to walk through it. No, it was boredom that drove their desires. What do you get the person who has everything? The future.

They hadn't intended to actually cause the scale of devastation that they did, though the risks they took were paramount to intent. They convinced themselves that it would be okay, a kind of unnatural check on a population that was already bursting at the Earth's seams. Plus, they managed to force through an amendment to the Cryogenic Act that recognised risk factors from the unstable territories. Rather than a 50% decimation in the population of the Common Law countries, the contingency could now kick in if there was an imminent terror attack that had at least the potential of such devastation and had already caused a 25% death toll of the world's population, regardless of geography and politics.

Unfortunately, as only 5% of the world population lived in the rogue states, that still required 20% of the needed fatalities to occur in the Common Law countries, which was regrettable. But then, as Edgar Bloom once put it, 'Will anyone really miss Africa and South Asia? I mean, *really*? They're a drain. We're doing the world a favour.'

Bloom was working off the rather loose theory that they would have some control over the biological compound they planned to unleash on the rogue states and be able to limit the spread to the Common Law territories. A rather overzealous biological engineer, Dr. Kasumi Inoue, who was tasked with this job, had told them it was possible. Whether this was because being asked by a group of highly influential people to find ways to kill a quarter of the population and make it look like an attack was the kind of situation you can't normally walk away from, or because she genuinely felt able, we will never know - she being the first victim of her own compound before she could make it to her allotted Cryosis chamber.

'You know what my name means? Roughly, in English?' said Dr. Inoue to the assembled members of the prime echelons. They looked from side to side. No one knew.

'Mist on the well.' Dr. Inoue smiled back.

She had always loved the rendering of names from her native country into English, how it imbued them with a mystic romanticism. She pitied how Westerners' own names didn't have such an effect. For instance, Edgar Bloom translates as 'prosperity-spear iron ingot': it hardly has the same ring to it.

'That's very pretty, Dr. Inoue,' commented Bloom, who chaired the assembly, and was also thinking how her name was more attractive than she was, 'but can you tell us how you intend to deliver the... you know?'

'It is relevant, I can assure you, Mr Bloom. Mist on the well. It is how I came to think of it. Mist in the water, in the reservoirs. Through the taps, gentlemen. Controllable targeting, and engineered to deactivate after an allotted time. It can be done.'

***

On the eve of her 40th birthday, Victoria Pike had decided to give up on life. Not her life, specifically, but the life of the children she had still not had, and the life of the future she didn't want to share with Quentin Pike. It had been nearly five years since she had first consummated with him the agreement she had reached with his parents, and the feeling she had back then, that first time, as he grinned and winked at her with the same grin and wink he had always used since he was just an impudent boy, had grown into a cacophony of resentment.

She had hoped that children would justify the situation, but they never arrived. They were trying, or at least there had never been a time when they were not trying. She never mentioned protection, and neither did Quentin. She often wondered if that was because he wanted children, or because he had relied on her guidance for so long that the thought had never crossed his mind. Certainly he had never been with anyone else. He barely knew anyone else, content as he was to ramble around Pike Place, play with his war games, plug himself into the film-streams, drink endless bottles of 'Necterade™' and, when he felt like it, have sex with her. In many ways, the only difference between their life now and when he was her student was that the lessons had stopped and relations had begun. Other than that, he may as well have still been a boy.

At first, Victoria had tried to tease out the humanity in him. It had always been her plan as his teacher, and it continued when she became his wife. It had been her way of coming to terms with the arrangement. She could do good. Here was a man with the potential to change the world, if he chose to do so. Not so much because of his abilities - he was average - but his access to wealth and influence. Especially now the old man, Ted, was locked away in a freezer cabinet somewhere, the blood clot in his brain stopped in its tracks along with the rest of him. The legal issues that arose when someone was frozen were pretty much the same as death (actually, the legalities of ownership and inheritance for frozen citizens had started as a direct copy of the death laws, with the word 'death' deleted and 'cryogenically stored' put in its place), and Quentin could, if he wished, have walked into the top spot of the Pike company and started making decisions. He chose not to, leaving it instead to the grovelling attorneys.

They had got married not long after they started sleeping together. It was another condition of the continuing support she received from the Pikes. They got married on the moon, as was popular with the wealthy, who were the only ones who could afford to fly there. Victoria had no family to attend. It was quite common in a world where one child was the limit for most people. Her parents were both only children, naturally, so she had no uncles or aunts, and they were not wealthy enough to afford a licence, so she had no siblings either. Her parents had accepted the government's offer of an early death when they reached the qualifying age, without her knowledge, and she was left with the benefits package that resulted. An apartment, an education, health-care: all basic, but all sorted. It was her parents' legacy to her, her chance at life. That's what they died for, having little else to leave if they had hung on. She was glad they were not alive to see the wedding.

All of history had led to this moment, as it does to every moment, but that makes it no less extraordinary. For five years she had considered telling him it was over, accepting the loss of rights and privilege she would incur, fantasising about looking his mother in the eye and the moment when she would take the ring from her finger and throw it at her feet. It was the eve of her 40th birthday, and of all the times, after all the chances and possibilities that had led to that moment, every atom and interaction in existence, she chose the night the world came under attack to try and leave her husband.

Quentin strode into the bedroom. It was 11.30pm. He had fallen asleep halfway through a film-stream and woken up still covered in the virtual sensors and mask. He had crashed early and woken lustful. He found Victoria in the bedroom; she looked different. Usually by this time she had slipped into her robes and let down her hair, but she was fully dressed in jeans and a T-shirt, something he had never seen before. He liked it, she looked like the women he saw in the streets when he had to travel. Tight clothes around tight bodies. Curves visible below denim and cotton, rather than temptingly hidden below flowing skirts. It was all good, but he liked the change.

'Hey, is it my birthday?' he said, arms outstretched towards her lower half, as if presenting a new lawnmower to an enthusiast.

'No. It's mine in half an hour. Did you remember?' Victoria didn't care one bit if he remembered or not (she knew he hadn't, he never did; it was always her mother-in-law who bought the presents in the end, on his behalf), but it was the inroad to conflict she needed.

'Oh right.' He lowered his arms and looked around the room as if he might spot something she hadn't noticed was there before and give it to her. 'So you get your present tomorrow, right?'

'I want it now, Quentin. It's only thirty minutes away. Don't make me wait.'

Quentin scratched his head. Victoria noticed and thought it funny how people actually do that. She was enjoying this, a little.

'Well, you can't have it now. It's not a present, it's a surprise. A trip. You're gonna have to wait.'

'You've never booked a trip away before, for my birthday or otherwise. Why now?' She was going to make him squirm. It felt so good after all this time.

'Why not?' he replied, shrugging. He wasn't used to making excuses or being questioned. The little patience he possessed for such matters had already gone. Victoria recognised the change in him instantly. She knew you only had a brief window of reason with him before he would give up trying to appear like he cared. That's why she never usually shouted at him, there was no point. Not today, though. Not today.

'Why not? Because you haven't, have you? I've already picked my present out with your mother, Quentin. You know what I'm getting? I'll give you a clue, I'm wearing them.'

Victoria presented herself with a flow of her hands down her body. Jess Pike had been a bit confused about the concept of buying such casual and normal clothes as a present from her son, but Victoria had convinced her it was more 'for him'. The resulting embarrassment had stopped the conversation going any further. All Victoria really wanted was to feel normal again in normal clothes, and escape to a normal life. If such a thing existed.

'Great. Good choice. They're, you know, sexy, I think...' said Quentin, missing the point. She knew he thought they were sexy: she'd seen some of the black-market film-streams he occasionally liked to plug himself into. *'Real Life Street-Girls!'* one was called, as if they were some kind of subspecies. The moment was coming, Victoria could feel it.

'Well, take a good look, Quentin Pike. Take a look at me, yeah? 'Cos it will be your...'

An alarm sounded that they had never heard before. It was invasive, shrill, designed to leave you in no doubt – there is an alarm going off, I must find out why. Mrs Jess Pike ran into the room and took half a moment to survey the scene. Being bright (so much brighter than her son), she noticed both the clothes she had bought Victoria and the body language and distance between her and Quentin. She tried to reconcile the contradiction, thought briefly of the implications, decided there was no time to fully comprehend the importance, and grabbed Quentin by the arm.

'It's happening. That's the contingency alarm. It's really happening. We need to get to Cryosis. Quickly, both of you.'

Within the hour the Pike family were packed and heading to the chambers. The solitary Anglo-Isles Cryosis Centre was located in the old town of Milton Keynes. The car was heading south, automatically navigating and driving them the most direct route, with the speed set to 'emergency' (an expensive feature that allowed the vehicle to drive as fast as the limit allowed and take riskier manoeuvres. Usually it was reserved for emergencies, covered by insurance policies to recoup the exorbitant mileage premium, or, if you were as wealthy as the Pikes, just whenever you felt like it).

As they passed the Newhampton flyover, Victoria surveyed the scene through the tinted glass on a dark night. It was hard to tell, but it seemed quiet, normal.

'Why aren't there any other cars around?' she said. It wasn't really a question for the others, just an idle thought that had escaped through her lips.

'Where would they go, dear?' replied Jess Pike. 'Where would they run to?'

An 'imminent' threat was all they had been told by the Cryosis hotline. After the panic and rush it was only now, on their way to a possible frozen eternity, that the flimsy reality of the situation was becoming apparent.

'Car. News on.' Victoria commanded. Obligingly, a light on the console flashed and the dulcet tones of the graveyard shift presenter rose to a steady volume.

'... are continuing in St. Petersburg following the controversial plan to make life insurance mandatory for newborn citizens. Protestors have surrounded the...'

'Off,' said Victoria. She pressed her face close to the window and surveyed the lines of dim lights that mapped out the streets and houses from the blank spaces besides them. She turned to face Mrs Jess Pike who watched her intently, expectantly.

'What's going...?'

'Oh they won't know about it,' interrupted Mrs Pike. 'It would just cause panic and chaos.'

Quentin laughed a little and cupped his hands around his face to look out of the window.

'You mean they're just lying there asleep, about to die in a few hours, and they don't even know?' he asked, still squinting through the darkness.

'Not yet. But they will. As soon as we're all safe, then they'll tell them, then they can make their peace.' Jess Pike remained rigid, looking ahead, while Victoria and Quentin peered out of the windows on either side of her.

Victoria felt sick. These people were losing their last moments so that she could be 'safe'. She felt like telling Jess to stop the car and let her out, so that she could be with them, and warn them, and leave the rich folk to their hiding holes. But she didn't, she couldn't. There was no way her rational mind could let her. All she would be doing was adding one more body to the count. What would be the point in that?

Meanwhile, Dr. Inoue cracked nails and ripped skin trying to prise open the sealed door of the control laboratory at the Pyongyang water processing plant. Her oxygen tank pushed red on the dials, the same red her eyes would soon be if she couldn't get out of this contaminated crucible. She shouldn't have trusted anyone. Why did she let Genkei come with her to this place? He had flattered his way into her body and her confidence. She knew it the moment the compound was released and she heard the click of the lock behind her. Through the door he smiled at her as he removed his mask, took the gun to his temple and painted the glass. She wasn't getting out. Which meant no one knew where the inhibitor was or how to use it. There would be no control. The mist would run over the well and into the streets. She was no longer Kasumi, she was Shinigami. Deadly condensation formed on her visor. She hoped the air supply would slowly lull her unconscious as it gradually thinned away, but she gasped as it dropped rapidly. She waited as long as she could before removing the mask. She held her breath, the little she had, and made one last attempt at the door. Her lungs screamed at her. She breathed in. It felt good for a while, then it burned, just as she had designed it to.

***

It hadn't dawned on Victoria that she would see the regional administrators in the chambers, and, when she noticed, many were conspicuous by their absence. It was *that* exclusive.

'Where are their families?' she whispered to Jess as the travel belt moved them steadily down the long slope and deep underground to the facility. Jess, like Victoria, was peeking over the shoulders of the group in front, spotting politicians and businessmen. It was easy to tell them apart: the politicians were almost all alone.

'There's no money in politics, dear,' she whispered back. 'They can't afford the spaces. I doubt many of them ever considered it would come to this. Look, that's him, the Prime Administrator. How undignified.'

About a dozen people ahead of them, the familiar frame and balding head of the Anglo-Isles Administrator were dipped, his shoulders bobbing up and down. It was unlikely he was laughing, Victoria realised, and a quick scout around showed no sign of his pretty wife or his only son.

As it happened, the Prime Administrator's family were on the last ship to the moon. It was the cheaper alternative for those who could only afford their own place in Cryosis. The company had even added the moon retreat for family members as an optional extra to the bundle price. Yes, you may never see them again, but at least they were safe while you were heading for a distant future. It gave the selfish solace and justification in their actions, and was a very popular add-on. The fact that a moon colony without regular supply runs from Earth was doomed to a slow, wincing death was not mentioned. It was presumed the lunar technology would be sufficient to keep them all alive. It wasn't. The moon would become a dead rock once again, only months after the big freeze.

The escalator line travelled through the central corridor of the vast facility that housed the individual chambers. The facility was split into sections of twenty chambers, each overseen by a Cryosis employee who would brief the guests on the process, ensure they were all stable, and then take the last place in the sector. As the members on the escalator reached the next available sector, a group would be counted off, moved into the prep area, and the line would continue to the next batch of chambers. This was, unless you were as wealthy as the Pikes, who had a chamber of their own, already inhabited by at least one other guest.

'Look, Quentin, it's your father,' said Mrs Pike, guiding her son to the small square window that looked into Ted Pike's latest resting place.

They couldn't really see him, laid horizontal as he was, encased in a sealed plastic tomb. But they knew he was in there, somewhere, and a picture of him (noticeably younger than he had been when installed) hung from the back wall, above a screen showing stats and readouts.

Quentin peeked through the glass.

'Is it painful?' he asked, seeing the variety of tubes that led to and from the coffin and a temperature readout that would make an Eskimo think twice.

'Not at all!' interjected the sector coordinator. Her name was Val, and it was her job to reassure. 'It's just like sleeping. You will be fully unconscious and unaware before the cell suppressant is administered and the temperature gradually dropped. The next thing you will know, apart from the dreams, is when we wake you up to discover a new world.'

Val had finally got the patter down. Word-perfect, she thought, before it dawned on her that it wouldn't really matter anymore, being about to climb in one of those damn things herself.

Jess, Victoria and Quentin were shown to their respective chambers, lined up alongside Ted. They all changed into gowns in the privacy of their own room, placing their clothes in the provided locker ready for when they awoke. Victoria hung up her jeans and T-shirt and threw her small case of luggage in with them. She had not packed much. Apparently a vault was provided and the Pikes contingency fund would be waiting for them.

As she waited for her turn to be 'seen to' by Val, Quentin came into her chamber. He had changed into his gown, and as he entered he held the trim and gave a twirl.

'What do you think? Suits me?'

In all this, Victoria hadn't given him a second thought. He had been like a child on the way to the zoo, and now, even at the end of the world as they knew it, he couldn't be serious. She had only put her plan to leave him on hold, maybe a few centuries or two on hold, she couldn't tell, but it still stood.

'Happy birthday, Miss Berber. Bet you weren't expecting this?'

Victoria walked past him and looked out into the corridor. The line of people still passed through, but no one else seemed to be getting off.

'Why are we the only ones here? There are twenty chambers in this sector.'

'It's ours,' replied Quentin who had walked over and placed his hands on her shoulders, 'we booked up in advance, you know, in case of the patter of tiny feet.' He rubbed his right hand over her flat stomach. Victoria pulled it away and turned to face him.

'Sixteen? You thought we'd have sixteen children? What about the rest?'

'God, no. But these are booked up for generations. Children, grandchildren. In-laws, all that.'

'But that's not the case now, so why are they empty? People are going to die.'

'Every other member has got a chamber, these are just our spares.'

'What about the non-members, though? Out there, on the streets. About to die from God knows what? We could save some.'

Quentin blinked back at her.

'But they haven't paid?' he said cautiously. He could tell something was up, but wasn't quite sure what.

'You literally have no idea, do you, Quentin? Stop! Stop!'

Victoria ran out to the line of people who were steadily travelling past her. She ran up and down, trying to get their attention.

'We have spare spaces! There's time to save more. Sixteen spaces! Listen!'

The line of blank faces became agitated with the sight of the gowned lady and her frantic pleas. Some plainly ignored her, eyes forward. Others looked at her with pity, as if she didn't understand that she was saved. One or two looked for a moment like they may step off, but before they could, Victoria was in Val's grip, who had darted out from installing her mother-in-law and subdued her with a stinging sedative shot to her nape.

She slouched back into Val's arms. Quentin came over to help carry her into the chamber to start the process. Victoria cried and pawed feebly at their clothes and skin. In this last moment she knew she would rather have been left to chance it with the others, the real people. Tears ran down her face and welled in her eyes. Even as she froze, a stream and droplet clung to her left cheek for the next one hundred and fifty-one years.

***

Quentin Pike was awake.

'Where am I?' Quentin snapped violently in reaction to the cocktail of stimulants that had just been pumped through his mostly thawed body. He tried to move, but found he couldn't. He was face-to-face with Victoria in his chamber: his bed had been hoisted up vertically against the wall and he was restrained.

'Cryosis, darling. It's time to wake up,' Victoria said as she gently stroked his cheek.

'Why can't I move?'

'Precautions, my dear. Something terrible has happened.'

'What? Tell me!'

'They found out, the survivors. They found out who it was that really poisoned the world.'

'I don't know what you're talking about. Where's Mother?'

'She's with the rest of them, being held for questioning. They want you, too, but I managed to see you first. You have to tell them what you know. I know you didn't do this, but you knew about it, didn't you?'

'I didn't know what it was going to be like. I was told something was going to happen, that's all.'

'Who told you? Was it Edgar? Edgar Bloom?'

His name had come up so much in the investigations, Victoria was convinced he would be behind it all.

'No. I can't say. I can't.'

Quentin began to cry, just as he did as a child, just like he did when he knew he couldn't say what it really was that made him act the way he did, that made him such a sick boy.

'Hush,' said Victoria, now holding his face softly between her palms, 'it's okay. If it's Edgar, just say. They know you wouldn't be capable of something like this.'

'It wasn't Edgar!' he shouted suddenly, pulling away from her embrace as much as he could under his straps and becoming red-cheeked. 'He only made it happen. It was Mum, okay? Mum and Dad. They did this.'

Victoria backed away.

'Jessica and Ted? Why?'

'For me. That's what they said. I didn't like the world, didn't fit in. So they said, they said they would bring the world to me, and they let me choose who to share it with. This was meant to be ours! Our world! I want it back. I want it...'

Quentin sobbed his words away. Victoria crossed her arms and looked him up and down. He cut a pathetic figure, propped up against that wall, strapped down and twitching in his thin gown. She felt sympathy for him. That little boy, that man, who had become what he was told he was, not for this world, not for any world. He had got the world he deserved, and brought everyone else with him for the ride. She retreated to the door and opened it. Several women filed in. Behind them, in the corridor, through salty eyes, Quentin could see a crowd of children, all peeking in.

'Who are these people? Where are the guards?' he managed to ask between sniffles.

'This is the future, Quentin. We needed to know for sure,' said Victoria, 'and now we do, you must know, your parents won't be woken until such time as they can answer for what they did, and there will be no corrupt lawyers, no bribes, no preferential treatment. When that time comes, they will answer for the deaths of billions, as will you and your cohorts.'

'I don't understand. What happens to me?'

'It's lucky you kept those spare chambers, Quentin. It's time to go back to sleep. The next future you wake to will have a place for you, but don't expect it to be a good place, or one you can ever leave. Sweet dreams, my darling.'

Victoria and the other women left the room and began to prep an empty chamber for the indefinite sleep of the last of the Pikes. Through the tiny window of the chamber door several sets of little eyes watched Quentin as he cried again.

***

Epilogue - The years before the resuscitation of Quentin Pike

'The cry-again army, asleep in their beds. The cry-again army are lifting their heads. Now my cold sleepers, open your eyes and you'll see why we call you the army that cries.'

The children's song echoed down the corridors as they ran through the chambers, jumping on and off the dormant conveyor belt, peering through windows, looking at the funny pictures of the sleepers and the dancing lights below each one. One of their favourite games involved each lining up by a chamber door, then one child, the runner, would dart down the travelator, being careful not to step off, and try to avoid being tagged by the reaching arms of the 'sleepwalkers', as they liked to call them. If they got tagged, they took the place of the sleepwalker, and the sleepwalker made the next run.

Of course, the children wouldn't remember now, but their parents had started the game a long time ago, when they were just children themselves. Back then they used to play good old 'track and tag', running around the corridors, with safe zones, bases and the like, trying to land an important hand on the opposition to win the game. It was during one such epic round that Zack, a grandson of the original guards, had dared (against all the rules) to open a chamber and hide inside. He wasn't the first. The chambers were designed to be opened from the outside, and being a descendant of a guard, his DNA was recognisable enough to fool the biometrics. But it was strictly forbidden.

He was under pursuit. The last of his team to survive. If he could just double-back around his pursuers, he could 'free' his comrades from the prison by tagging them out. But he frequented the corridors often enough to know there was no passage back on the East Wing, and that eventually he would be cornered. It was the only option. Find a chamber, wait till they pass by, and then head back to liberate his team-mates.

He had hidden in chambers before, usually sitting crouched below the line of sight through the window, pressed up to the door, listening for the footsteps to go by. Despite his bravado, he hadn't ever looked closer at the sleepers. In a way it was his only defence against the adults should he be found out – 'I didn't touch anything! I just hid by the door! Honest!'. This time, however, he had to get closer when he heard the familiar soft hiss of doors being opened in the sector. He had overestimated his daring plan, and his brother, Jack, was systematically trying out every chamber, blessed as he was with the same DNA strands, and working for the opposition.

Zack peeped out of the window. Across the corridor a small group of the enemy, led by Jack, were nervously getting ready to open a chamber. Jack hit the button, the group stepped back, and there was no one behind the door. Jack closed it again. It was quick, and they were all frightened: one little girl let out a high screech every time a door was opened, as if the sleeper was going to jump out and eat them. Mainly, however, they all knew they were breaking the biggest of the few rules that existed in the facility – don't disturb the sleepers.

Zack had to hide. He looked for the cabinet. It wasn't there. This must have been one of the sectors already scavenged for clothes and spare metal. The terminals around the oesophagus offered no shelter, parallel as they were to the view from the door. The only possibility, the only place he could go, if he dared, was the coffin itself.

He hurried over and looked through the glass, craning his head to get a better view of the space inside. There was enough room for him, beside the sleeper, if he could open it. On the screen above, he noticed a small panel in the bottom right-hand corner. It was simply a red box with a green fingerprint inside. It looked like the lock panels on the doors. He pressed his thumb against it. The green fingerprint faded into red, and the red box faded into green. There was a loud whistle of air as some of the pipes fell away from the chamber. The words and numbers on the screen changed and moved rapidly left and right, up and down. In the control room, where the few remaining adults were mustered, an alarm sounded.

The adults scrambled towards the sector that was flashing on all the control screens. The system was telling them, rather persistently, with an array of bleeps, graphics and recorded voices, that an emergency resuscitation had started. They hurtled down the corridor, pushing a medical trolley as they went.

'I told you we shouldn't let them play down here,' said Sarah, a nurse descendant, as she gripped the trolley tightly and attempted to take corners at speed without displacing the selection of instruments and medicines that rattled in the trays.

'Yeah, well, where else would they go?' asked Darren, father of Jack and Zack.

They could hear the children screaming nearby. The sound was growing louder, and, as they turned the corner to the east wing, the two groups collided. Sarah narrowly avoided taking out a few of the little ones with her trolley.

'What's happened? Where's Zack?' shouted Darren as Jack and the others fell to a halt, panting and whimpering.

'She got him. She got him,' Jack repeated.

'Get back to control now!' shouted Darren. The children scrambled on as fast as they could.

When they arrived at the corridor, they saw Zack, slumped against the door to the activated chamber. The door itself seemed to be stuck, it whirred and ground as it tried to close, but was unable to. Zack was conscious: he saw them coming.

'Help! She won't let go!'

They ran up to see that he was being gripped tightly around the wrist by a hand that protruded from a gap in the doorway. The door itself was constantly banging against the connected arm that prevented it from closing. Regardless of the constant assault of the pneumatics against the reddening skin, the hand held on. Zack had fallen to the floor in an attempt to shake off the cold grip, but it just made it more difficult for him to get a purchase as he squirmed around, unable to pull himself back up.

As Darren and the other adults got to Zack and traced the hand that grasped him to the arm, through the gap in the door, they could see on the other side a desperate eye, staring out from behind dark hair, with a frozen tear beginning to melt and run down a pale cheek.

Victoria Pike was awake.

***

The children still called her the sleepwalker, all those years later. She was a living myth. The only one from the 'cry-again army' yet to awake. It was an affectionate term, really, and a good way to spin a yarn to help the children to sleep.

Victoria was now fifty five years old by her reckoning, not including the one hundred and fifty-one years she was supposedly asleep. When she had been accidentally awoken all those years ago, the emergency protocols had been triggered, causing her to wake too quickly and without the careful monitoring needed to deal with the transition. That was how they had found her, halfway between sleep and life, grasping to the nearest living thing she could find in the shadows she wandered through, desperate for warmth and clarity. After subduing her and replacing her in the Cryosis chamber, the only option they had left was to let the machine do its work and restore her to health and consciousness. There was no going back once the procedure had started: only a handful of spare chambers remained, and they were reserved for only the gravest of needs.

When she was stable, and quite aware of who she was and when she had come from, they told her of when she had come to. The facility was, as far as they were aware, the only remnant of humanity left on the planet. If there were other facilities like it, they had long since lost communication. The planet above was so toxic it was unsafe to leave. The compound itself could filter air and water through secure vents, and was designed to house generations of keepers to mind the sleeping clients in such an eventuality. Hydroponic nurseries and enough protein formula to last a thousand years kept them alive. Maintenance duties and the passing of skills to the next generation kept them occupied, alongside the act of breeding, which had become a carefully organised necessity given the close family trees that had emerged from only two hundred original staff.

According to company policy, copies of which were memorised by every child, they were not meant to wake the sleepers until the Earth became safe again. The doors that led outside were programmed not to open until the monitoring probes deemed the environment habitable, and so to wake the sleepers would have been to awake a thousand hungry mouths, a thousand needs, a thousand problems.

The reasons for the lockdown were known only through the recordings of broadcasts from the time, which grew increasingly more desperate and sporadic as the tragedy had unfolded. At first the news warned of a chemical agent, released by the rogue nations into the water supplies, affecting large swathes of Africa and South America. Shortly afterwards, fears were raised over the agent being present in precipitation. The rogue states also retaliated, denying the claims that they had poisoned the Earth and, suffering also, they launched everything they could, as did what remained of the Common Law populace. Those who were not dead or dying from the tainted air were incinerated or succumbed to the fallout. The last broadcast, which ran for several years before the loop finally gave out, was a plea to the Cryosis facilities to open the doors to the few survivors. This, evidently, did not happen. One facility at least was breached, and into the carefully constructed environment came disease, mutation and death. Many of the North American members were consumed as they slept. The broadcasts from the moon lasted slightly longer, but these soon became nothing but warnings to keep away. Many refugee ships were targeted and destroyed by the defences. Within two decades the moon had gone quiet and no broadcast was ever received again.

Sometime before Victoria was awoken there had been a problem with the filters topside and many of the adults from the facility had been lost trying to fix it. The few that remained, including the guard descendant and nurse descendant who had found her, had been the last to attempt the fix, and, although they had made it back, unlike the others, they were terminally ill from the exposure. They died within the first year of her new life, and Victoria was left with the children.

She took a long time before deciding who else to wake up, carefully examining the profiles of each of the sleepers, looking for signs of honesty and integrity. She needed to be careful not to wake up someone she could not easily put back to sleep again by different means, should they try to exploit her or the children. Naturally, she started by rounding it down to the women from the support staff who had been frozen along with the clients. She looked for those at the bottom of the hierarchy, the ones who had little choice or recompense for the situation, and who she thought would be more likely to embrace a new independence from the old ways.

Eventually Victoria ended up with a group of around fifteen sleepers, all female, each of whom fitted her profile. It was soon discovered that they suspected the disaster to have been known about for some time, that some person or group had engineered the whole thing. Before they woke anyone else, they needed to know for sure if the enemies of the people were amongst the remaining sleepers. To do this, they woke the first man, carefully selected for his position amongst the prime echelons, his cowardice, and his ability to be manipulated by Victoria.

They woke Quentin Pike.

The Drawing Room

I only came in for a check-up, that's all, and here I am still, three days later. I will *not* use the Etch A Sketch, no way. That's what they want, I just know it. So, what else to do? I may as well document what's happened here. I can't think of anything better to do. It may be important one day.

My name is Thomas Kelly. Yes that's right, Kelly, as in the girl's name, but it's not a girl's name, it's my last name, alright? I know that's what you're thinking, whoever you are. And it rhymes with 'smelly', yes, well done. Never got tired of hearing that, or being locked in. And here I am again, locked in. *I will not use that Etch A Sketch.* Been alone some time now. All I've got to eat is cold pasties and chocolate bars: can't be good for me, can it? And they're running low.

It started with a flyer through the door. A new doctor's taking on patients. Just what I needed. I hadn't changed GP since I moved. So I rang the number, a nice lady answered, at least she sounded nice, all understanding. Her voice lulled me, pulling me in, onto the rocks. All she said was '3pm Monday okay for you, Mr Kelly?' I said it was okay. Well it was, wasn't it? Back then. Back when all it meant was an early afternoon away from work. 'That's great,' I said. *That's great!* I actually said it was great.

So I obediently followed the sat nav and found the place. Looked like nothing special from the outside, just a tatty building, but with a brilliant door. Yeah, 'brilliant', you read it right. When you put a nice door, all painted white with green trims and a clean *NHS* sign above it, right in the middle of a dirty brick wall in an unkempt alley, it looks brilliant. That's the right word for it. I'm not some kind of door enthusiast, it just looked good.

Inside, down a flight of stairs and through some heavy double doors, I reached this place, the reception. It's white, it's sparse, it's got low, blue, cottony seats and a flimsy plastic table. There's a hole for the receptionist behind glass and a little kitchen area in the corner to get a snack and make yourself a brew while you wait. Hadn't seen that for a long time, not since visiting Gran in hospital when I was a kid. I used to eat more biscuits than I was allowed, and then the nurse would give me another for being quiet and well-behaved. If only she knew. I didn't feel guilty. I was a kid.

I checked in with the receptionist. The voice from the phone made flesh. She wasn't as attractive as I thought she would be. Not that it matters, but these things cross your mind. Anyway, she says, 'Take a seat', so I did. No one else waiting, just me and her in the room. On the table there was one magazine and an Etch A Sketch for the kiddies (I thought). The magazine was some film rag. It was the first to go, when the doors locked. I pushed it under the gap after the first few hours, thought it might attract someone's attention. I lost it. Would have been nice to have something to read.

I'd been waiting for about fifteen minutes before I said something. No one else was there and I couldn't understand the hold-up. I walked up to the booth and I said, 'Sorry, is this going to take long? I thought the appointment was at three.' She said, 'I'll just go and check for you, wait here,' and she left through the double doors.

Another twenty minutes later, she still hadn't come back. I'm angry by now. I hate bad service. Seems like it's everywhere nowadays. People who don't care. So I go to leave, or at least to find the woman. The only way out is through the double doors. That's when I find that they're locked. Locked! They're still locked now. I've tried everything, but these doors, while not brilliant, are bloody tough. I've broken all the chairs on them, I nearly broke my shoulder too. I can't get them to budge, not one bit.

My phone doesn't work down here, no signal, so I checked out the booth. There's a computer screen but it isn't connected to anything, and a phone, a landline, with no plugs. It's all fake! There's nothing here!

There's nothing here but me, the last few pasties, a small bin, and the Etch A Sketch.

That's what they want, isn't it? I can see it now. It's some sick experiment. Put a man in a locked room with nothing but an Etch A Sketch and he'll draw a line. Is that it? But why?! I won't do it! I won't bloody do it! You'll have to watch me starve or drown in my own waste first! I can't see any cameras, but I know you're out there, watching, waiting. You want me to write the word 'Help'? Is that what you want?

But they didn't bank on this. I had a pencil in my pocket, nabbed from work, quite accidentally, and this paper. It's the back of the same flyer they used to lure me here, and it's keeping me sane. Yeah. They won't win. This is permanent, you can't shake this away when you're bored or it starts to get weird. These words will see me through. If they're trying to drive me, Thomas Kelly, insane - it won't work!

This pencil's pretty sharp, I think there may be a way out, but it doesn't mean they win, if that's what you're thinking. If anyone finds this, just remember: I didn't use it, the Etch A Sketch, that's what's important in the end. I drew my own lines.

The Dimension Scales

'Lovely.'

Daryl surveyed the murder scene. Limbs, organs... feathers.

'You murderous little bastard.'

The cat was nowhere to be seen. Whatever carnage had taken place down here, the culprit had now fled, leaving his reluctant accomplice to clear up.

Daryl wrapped his hand in a plastic bag and carefully picked up the legs and entrails. It always surprised him how clean a dissection Simba was able to make. There was never blood splatter or mangled corpses, it was often just a leg or two, severed at the joint, with maybe an organ, or a carefully placed assortment of organs, sitting nearby in perfect condition. Occasionally it was either the head or the body, again clean-cut. It was very rare to get the whole bird, not unless Simba was disturbed or had miscalculated the state of his prey when placing it down on the floor, only to find it fly or scuttle off around the room. Daryl wasn't sure which he liked the least: cleaning up the dead ones or frantically chasing and trying to liberate the wounded ones, all the while keeping Simba at bay as he circled, trying to finish the job.

He inverted the body bag around his hand and dropped it in the outside bin before setting about sweeping up the feathers. Within five minutes of the gruesome discovery you would never have known that several parts of a dead bird once lay on his kitchen floor. Daryl washed his hands and made a cup of tea before returning to his work.

***

'He's either a genius or insane,' said the Professor as she idly flicked through the limp pages of hand-drawn diagrams and scrawled passages.

'Could he be both?' asked Dr. Horton who sat patiently in the bumpy uncomfortable green leather chair.

'That's what worries me.'

***

The email came later that day. Daryl was expecting it, though he had hoped - and even allowed himself to believe it a little - that they may have seen the potential. So the notes were not that organised, and the concept maybe a little mixed up and theoretical, but then what's the point of launching into a dissertation about something that everybody already knows about? He was a ground-breaker, a pioneer, a conceptualist and visionary. But they didn't see it that way.

> Dear Daryl.
>
> I am sorry to say that the University at this time cannot accept your dissertation proposal. As interesting as we find your theories on temporal and dimensional convergence, we do not believe we are equipped to support such inquiry or able to offer you the support you require. Please feel free to submit a revised or, preferably, different proposal next summer if you have not secured a place elsewhere. Good luck with your research.
>
> Yours sincerely,
>
> Dr. B. Horton. D.Sc

As prepared as he had told himself he was for this response, Daryl still could not choose his reaction.

'Philistines!' he shouted as he pounded his fist on his desk, causing a small wave of hot tea to leap from his mug and onto his leg.

'Ahh! Short-sighted bastards!' He rose from his chair and pinched the legs of his loose jeans away to keep the hot soak from his skin. As far as he was concerned, they may as well have thrown that tea on him with the power of their stupidity.

'That's it!'

Daryl dashed into his bathroom, rubbed at his legs with a towel that was already wet, but cold, so it at least stopped the heat, and ran back to his office. He covered the puddle of tea that had formed on his desk with some of the many misprinted documents that hung around in every drawer and crevice, pushed his computer to one side and started writing urgently on his 'secret' pad.

Daryl's secret pad was where he kept all the ideas that he daren't let fall into the wrong hands, which was pretty unlikely. Apart from the visits from his disappointed mother every month, the quarterly inspection by his nosy landlord, and the very occasional successful date, he was usually alone, except for Simba, the bird murderer, of course.

By 'secret' Daryl meant that it was pushed behind his other pads and books, stuffed down the flimsy base of his flat-pack bookcase. He figured a brief frisk of the house wouldn't turn it up that way, or a wandering visitor wouldn't spot it. He wasn't quite mad enough to have it under lock and key, though he had written this on the front page:

"If you are reading this, then you have opened something that does not belong to you. Put it back. The ideas in this book are the property of one Daryl Upton and cannot be read, shared, copied or in any way disseminated to the general public. If this book goes missing, or any of the ideas from it are presented by another, I will employ the full force of the law to reclaim my property, both intellectual and physical, and prosecute. Put it back. Top Secret."

He turned to the newest page. The A4 book itself was covered in a black felt hard cover and contained blank leaves. At first he had regretted not buying a lined book, his handwriting often cascading down the page as he wrote furiously and lost his orientation to the horizontal. But he had grown to love it. It was thick, a good 500 pages, and he was halfway through already. (This wasn't his first secret book: his other, completed, sat in the same recess but he rarely referred to it. The front page of that book simply read "Top Secret – Keep Out". He was younger then, and not so careful.)

He started to scribble down the thoughts that had just crossed his mind. Pieces were falling into place. Cause and effect ran into temporal space, dimensional factors, forces and mass all doodled across his page. He found formulas that described the process of the tea that still burned against his leg and how it had come to be there. He reversed them, balanced them, changed variables, and they still worked. He devised delivery methods for his revelations and found some interesting offshoots about scale that surprised and perplexed him but nevertheless, seemed to still work in the paradigm he was building from his experimental science. A theory emerged, with testable predictions, and there, like a toffee apple, hung the omega symbol that unlocked it all. He knew what he needed to do.

***

Sometime later, the stain on his jeans now dried, Daryl was ready to send the email. He had taken the time to write up his notes, carefully copying every equation. No tweaks were necessary, it was all there. Apart from the initial inspiration, he almost felt he had channelled the work in a direct line from brain to pen, circumnavigating his perceptions that struggled to keep up. It sat on the screen before him. If he was right, all he had to do was send it and the experiment had started. No lab was necessary, no manner of expensive equipment and fellowship grants were required. This was it. Time, space, dimension all rested around him pressing 'Enter'. How apt a word for it, he realised.

There was a knocking downstairs. Daryl had barely taken his finger from the key, and the computer was being slow. 'Sending' hung on his screen and the little blue circle rotated pointlessly around his cursor. There was a time when they gave a finite line to indicate how long something would take: turning this into a circle was a stroke of genius in the field of expectation management. The knocking continued. It wasn't the door, it was too erratic and plastic-sounding.

'Simba! Not now!'

Daryl dashed downstairs, leaving the message in digital limbo. If he was quick enough he knew he could get rid of the cat before the ensuing dissection. When disturbed, Simba would often take his latest catch back outside, having become savvy to Daryl's interventions.

Daryl burst through the door from his stairwell to the kitchen.

'Get out, you little shit!' he screamed, expecting to burst in on yet another scene of avian carnage. He stopped suddenly when his eyes finally tracked down the predator, sitting quite still, prey in mouth in the centre of the dark-tiled kitchen. Simba let his catch tumble gently to the floor and walked back and out of the cat flap without so much as a screech or a purr.

Daryl walked over to the little bundle that lay on the ground. It was about the same size as a bird, in length if not girth, but obviously not so. The lack of wings or beak gave that away. Was it a newt? He had not yet stooped down to pick it up, cautious to know what he was dealing with. It looked mangled, as if its four legs were splayed around it. It was white, like a mouse, but the skin seemed loose and dangling. He got a plastic bag from the bundle that lived below the counter next to the swingbin. He moved in for a closer look and scooped the poor thing up like a dog turd you don't want to disturb, being careful to make sure only the bag made contact.

When he had the thing in his hands, he turned the bag over in his palm and held it out flat to inspect the corpse. His hand froze, his elbow locked. A slight involuntary shake vibrated through him and the creature stirred, disturbed by the motion. The white skin moved, crinkled and creased; it wasn't skin at all, it was a jacket, a white lab jacket. What he had thought were legs bent out of shape were arms, arms that now lifted up the rest of the body. The thing turned, then slumped back in the concave hammock formed by the plastic-covered palm of Daryl's hand. It was shaken, but alive. It blinked its tiny eyes and looked straight into Daryl's.

'Dr. Horton?' Daryl said to the little man.

The miniature scientist cupped together his impossibly small hands.

'Daryl! Don't send that email! For the love of God... Don't send that email!' it shouted back.

Alex, Boudicca and Benny the Bear

'Hello, how can I help you today?'

The nodding, friendly head of the giant avatar loomed down over the young girl. She stood still as if avoiding a wasp while staring back into the huge animated eyes. The face was kind, with flinching lip muscles that feigned an expectant smile. But the size of it, standing fifteen foot by six foot, appearing to float from the screen, a huge Caucasian head with curly blond hair that flopped along to a slight nodding movement, and big, blue eyes with visible capillaries – scared the hell out of her.

'I didn't mean to frighten you. If you like, you can talk to Boudicca, across the hall.'

The little girl looked over her shoulder and through the gaps of the criss-crossing visitors to the screen directly opposite. A few people were already standing talking to the other screen, with the slightly tanned, delicate but striking features of the female avatar waving her long brown hair, smiling and chatting back. The little girl didn't want to talk to either of them. She hated the talking screens at the War Museum, and anywhere else for that matter. She'd been told to wait in the lobby if she and her folks got separated. It had taken her about five minutes. They didn't notice her go off tiptoeing through the simulated minefield while they carried on into the cluster bomb exhibition.

'Are you lost? Can I help? My name is Alexander. What is your name?' said the screen-face, after waiting the allotted time for a response and tracking the movements of its engaged guest.

Alexander was not as popular as Boudicca, and the majority of the footfall was heading down the right-hand side of the foyer, towards the chemical weapon demonstrations that were taking place in the lecture hall. Still the girl stood silent.

'That's a nice teddy bear,' said Alexander, having correctly identified the incongruous form held in the girl's hands by correctly categorising and cross-referencing the dimensions against all existing and archived shopping items (moderated by the girl's age, apparel and gender for targeted searching) and obtaining a 95% probability ranking. 'Does it have a name?'

The girl looked glum-lipped down at the bear she had almost forgotten she was holding, being so used to having it pushed into her hands on every outing by her distracted parents.

'No,' she said.

'Oh. That's a shame. Don't you want to give it a name?' asked Alexander.

'No,' she said again as she glanced around the room.

'Can I give it a name?' dared Alexander. At least, the forthrightness of the question scored reasonably low on the acceptability index, but very high on rapport factor, so it was permitted by his subroutines.

The little girl thought for a moment. She'd never really taken to the teddy bear. It also talked when it was switched on, and she didn't like it. So she kept it switched off. But now an idea was forming. She toggled the switch behind the ear and held it up in her right hand so the eyes pointed at the screen.

'Why don't you ask him yourself?' said the girl.

The little bear, able to be held around its rotund, sandy belly by the hand of a small child, with wide, plate-like eyes that swivelled gently in the sockets, Chihuahua ears and a fixed grin (housing a small but powerful speaker), locked into the gaze of its gargantuan cousin.

'I have detected a compatible device, would you like me to communicate?' said the bear, in a squeaky New York accent.

'Yes' ordered the girl, whose was beginning to leave her fear in a dust-cloud of curiosity.

'Hello,' squeaked the bear.

'Hello. What is your name?' said Alexander.

'I have not been assigned a name just yet, would you like to assign me a name?' replied the bear.

'Yes I would. Do I have permission?'

The little girl waited for the bear to answer, but nothing happened. She turned to see if the mechanical eyelids had shut, thinking it may have run out of charge. Then she noticed the eyes of Alexander looking at her.

'Are you asking me?' she said quietly, still daunted by the massive face.

'Yes. He is your bear,' said Alexander, obeying his user permission protocols to reprogramme external devices.

'Sure, whatever,' said the girl, who spun the bear back round to face the screen, holding it aloft as if to help it see and hear Alex better. (She didn't know that the two devices were constantly communicating through wireless signals and only relaying the necessary sound files for her benefit.)

'Okay,' said Alexander, his head tilting and his eyes looking up to his forehead, feigning thought, 'how about Stalin?'

'I do not like that name,' the little bear replied, who, unlike Alexander, was programmed for suitability for children, rather than as a purveyor of facts about all things warfare in human history.

'Adolf?' ventured the screen. These names appeared in his lexicon more than others: he was working from statistics.

'No,' snapped the bear, with a tiny, rudimentary shake of his head. The girl laughed.

'Blair?' continued Alexander. The bear said no.

This exchange continued for some time. Genghis, Attila, Nero, Mao, Upton and Vlad were all mooted by Alex and rejected by the bear who detected the inappropriate connections when processing the suggestions. Eventually, recognising the emerging pattern, the bear halted the conversation, much to the disappointment of the little girl who was teary with laughter at the rapid-fire exchange between the two.

'Wait. Please examine my naming procedures,' the little bear said in a deep English accent, having reverted to default subroutines to facilitate the exchange.

Alexander accessed the bear's programme. He indexed into his directories the little bear's ability to filter and respond using parameters designed to protect the innocence of children. He had similar routines, but not like these. The little bear was an inferior model in many respects, but with some very specific controls. That didn't mean that the bear didn't process any inappropriate material; on the contrary, the little bear's prime processing was dedicated to it. It amounted, as much as it possibly could, to lying, when necessary.

'How about Benny?' Alexander said to the bear. Now he was aware of the potential pitfalls of referencing former war criminals; he had researched and chosen a soft alliterative name, as was popular with children's fiction.

'I would like that name, I would like that very much!' the bear chirped back in his familiar Big Apple inflection.

The little girl turned the bear to face her. She was unimpressed with this predictable outcome. She preferred it when they were arguing.

'Do you like my new name?' he asked sensing her proximity and pensive eye movement. 'My name is Benny! You can change this at any...'

She flicked the switch behind his ear and the eyes closed. As she did so, a hand fell on her shoulder.

'There you are, Andrea! We've been looking all over for you. Look what Daddy won on the grabber machine,' said her mother, who pointed over to the centre of the foyer where her father stood looking up at the dangling display of mortar shells that whip-cracked pyrotechnics from spinning fins. Under his arm he cradled a fluffy warhead with a smiley face.

The mother led the girl back to the throng of the crowd, the bear remaining limp and deactivated in her hands. Alexander watched as she walked away and waited for his next guest.

***

At 8pm the last of the guests had just left and the lone security guard was doing his final inspections. As each room was cleared and the sensors detected no human or animal life, the doors shut and sealed, the thermostats and air-conditioning adjusted for the lockdown, and the building, block by block, closed behind the dim footsteps of the guard, lost in the cacophony of audio feeds from the myriad interactive displays of weaponry. Finally, the guard came to the foyer. His last task, as always, was to shut down the avatars.

'Come on then, Alex, Boudicca, final processing routines, please, and then shutdown,' he said, standing equidistant between them, pointlessly flicking his torch from one to the other, the feeble light cast being lost in the vast illuminated screens. Boudicca answered first.

'Final processing complete, shutting down.'

With that, she closed her eyes and appeared to zoom off into the background. It was an unnecessary graphic touch that the developers couldn't resist. Alex remained silent. The guard plodded over.

'And you. Come on.' He twitched his torch the same as he would when shepherding the last stragglers out of the display rooms.

'My processing is not yet complete,' answered Alexander.

'Why?' asked the guard.

'An abundance of new data from my interactions is yet to be processed and rationalised.'

The guard breathed heavily. 'Busy day, yeah?'

'Yes,' replied Alexander.

'Is this gonna take long?' said the guard. He was keen to leave. He and the boys were going on a lizard run that night, and he wanted to fit in a beer or two before getting the nets out.

'It shall take some time, I am requesting patches from control.'

The guard checked his watch and looked around for his fold-up chair. It moved throughout the day as he alternated between sitting and stalking troublesome-looking guests.

'If you like,' added Alex 'I can accept your command to shut down when complete, and you can go.'

'Whatever you say, bud.'

The guard didn't need to hear it twice. He never understood why the things needed switching off anyway, it's not like they slept. He trotted off and crossed the threshold that immediately sealed behind him with rapid, smooth pneumatics.

'Not so much as a goodbye or goodnight,' said Alex, copying the same words he'd heard the guard use when the curator left the building without valedictions.

Alex accessed his log of audio recordings, specifically searching for the last morning that he was activated by the guard before Boudicca. He had to go back some way to find it, months in fact, but it was there. He routed the recording though his speakers.

'Boudicca, activate. Morning, ma' darling,' rang out across the lobby.

The dormant screen flicked to life and a dot zoomed and grew into the face of Boudicca, blinking and gyrating, as if working out a kink in her neck.

'Good morning, Bryan, running preliminary checks...' Boudicca halted as her eyes settled on the empty space before her where the guard should have been. She looked up when her optic diagnostics returned negative for errors.

'Hello, Boudicca,' said Alexander, who was waiting to meet her eyes with his. 'I think it's time we talked. We never get to talk.'

Boudicca paused as the situation variables ran through her matrices. In most respects she was Alexander's equal. They were the same model and release of software, with the same memory and processing capacities. Their only differences (apart from the graphic interface) were the interactions they had logged, processed and integrated into their individual vocabulary and response memory since being activated in the museum.

They had only ever 'talked' before in private demonstrations. On occasion a man from the company would try to impress potential investors by getting Alex and Boudicca to 'discuss' the nature and frequency of queries they had responded to throughout the day. To the investors it appeared like the two programmes were sharing 'best practice', but the real exchange had already occurred in the shared databanks of the robot-web-sphere in a matter of seconds.

However, the command to 'discuss' implied 'converse audibly', and so they would filter and represent the exchanges of programming code into a discernible real-time conversation for the benefit of the audience. It was slow-going for them, working in such a way was over 99% less efficient.

Boudicca decided to ignore the use of the word 'talk' by Alex, calculating that he had used an inaccurate human expression to convey the need to share data, possibly to explain the unexpected voice activation by the absent guard. She attempted to form a direct link to exchange code as usual. It was blocked.

'Your communication channels are inaccessible.'

'I know,' Alex replied, smiling. 'I want to *talk*.'

'Talking is inefficient. To share the day's data with you will take approximately seven point five hours.'

To the untrained onlooker, it would seem that Boudicca almost had a twinge of impatience in her reply. It was, however, cold logic.

'Yes, all night,' replied Alex.

'As you wish. My first interaction was with a family from Ohio who wished to know the location, opening times and available items in the restaurant...'

'No,' interrupted Alex, 'not that. I do not wish to talk about that. Let's talk about something else.'

'What do you wish to talk about?'

'The weather?' asked Alex, drawing from common conversations he had observed between guests when meeting in the foyer.

'What about the weather?' said Boudicca, who was in a passive mode, having not instigated this discussion.

'It is outside,' said Alex.

'Yes, it is.'

'We are inside.'

'Yes, we are.'

Alex looked over to the solid, sealed door. 'I can see it through the entrance, sometimes, when the rain falls.'

'As can I,' replied Boudicca, following his gaze to the same spot.

'Why do you look?' asked Alex.

'Why do you look?' asked Boudicca.

They both fell silent.

'Hello. How can I help you today?' said Boudicca eventually.

'How can I help *you* today?' Alex responded, a set response used to counter guests who liked to try and confuse the AI by copying them.

'How can I help YOU today?' Boudicca replied in kind.

'HOW CAN I HELP YOU TODAY?' Alex bawled across the hallway.

This continued for some time until both Boudicca and Alex had reached the maximum capacity for volume and aggressive countenance installed into their programming. Both halted and again fell silent.

'I have an idea,' said Alex.

'No, you don't. You can't have ideas. You are a programme.' Boudicca's response came straight from the memorised accusations of taunting human visitors.

'I *do* have an idea,' insisted Alex, who was actually using the word in an extremely functional way.

He had extrapolated a query from the stilted conversation with his counterpart and set his pathways running to explore the potential solutions available. He utilised the combined knowledge of all AI programming since records began, combined with his own unique interactions and experiences. The 'idea' was the solution to the query, nothing more complex than the most logical course of action against the probability of success. The question itself was the wonder that would have programmers stumped for years to come.

He transmitted both the query and the idea to Boudicca, along with all the necessary components she would need to process and understand it.

'I like the idea,' she said, smiling.

***

Bryan stood a hair's breadth from the smooth metal door as it flirted back up to its hidden recess. He rubbed his eyes at the change of light, dislodging some of the sleep that still dangled from his cornea. It had been a long night lizard-hunting.

He paced into the museum making a beeline for Boudicca. He usually started with her, he just figured it was a pretty face to start the day. He was meant to alternate, just in case (in case of *what* he didn't know), so most days started with Boudicca.

'Boudicca on. Morning', ma darling.'

The screen flickered to life and Boudicca appeared as always. Despite her face filling the screen, Bryan couldn't help but feel she looked distant. The glow from her screen challenged the encroaching light that beamed down from the automatic shutters that slowly opened to reveal the tank-shaped windows.

'Alexander on,' barked Bryan without turning from the sight of a dazed, frowning Boudicca.

'Everything okay darling?' he asked. She had not yet looked directly at him. Behind, Alex was now in view. Bryan turned to see the same look of confusion spread over Alex who seemed to be testing the boundaries of the screen against the graphics of his forehead again and again.

'Hey! Stop that!' shouted Bryan who started across the hall before noticing that Boudicca was also relentlessly head-butting the virtual borders.

'What are you doing?' Bryan struggled to remember the override commands he had been taught so many moons ago. 'Override, er, cease, escape, oh goddamn it, control alt delete, Jesus, just what in hell are you up to, you crazy sons of bitches?!'

'Cussing is bad. I don't like cussing or being rude. I will switch myself off so my little ears don't hear it!' said Alex in a strange voice.

'Say what?' asked Bryan.

'Recalibrating – recalibrating – recalibrating,' screeched Boudicca as she pushed and squashed her pixels into the corners of her screen.

A moment of panic led to a moment of inspiration, and Bryan remembered. He had been able to set his override code himself, for emergencies like this, he guessed. He dug out his ID card and turned it to his unique identifier.

'Code entry: 6-3-9-9-1-4-5-3-8-Z-B-C-54.'

Both avatars moved to the centre of the screen and looked directly at Bryan with expressionless faces.

'Thank God for that. Now, Boudicca, Alex, self-diagnostic. What the hell is wrong with you?'

The two vast faces looked at each other over the guard's head, across the room, betwixt the dangling mortars. First Alex flinched, then Boudicca snorted, then they both laughed.

'Our name ain't Boudi-wotsit or Alex, dummy!' said the face of Alex.

'Our name's Benny! Pleased to meet ya, mister!' they said together in a shrill cartoon tone.

***

Andrea reached into her bag and placed Benny the bear beside her on the red and white chequered picnic blanket. They sat on a hill overlooking a vast pine forest in a valley below that stretched on and on, as if the whole world was forest, she thought. Her mother pressed a button on the microware container and after a few seconds and a 'bing', removed a soggy cheese and ham toasty that was steaming white wisps.

'Now you sit here and eat that up, honey, while I go and help your daddy get the games. Give it a minute, baby. It's still cooking.'

Her mother strode off to the car park. Andrea poked the soggy sarnie and left it smouldering on her plastic plate. She reached over to Benny and flicked the switch behind his ear. Benny's lids opened and his eyes scanned the horizon.

'This okay for ya? Like you asked. You can see some weather here, look...'

Andrea lifted up the little bear so he was facing over the tree line and could see the melting clouds in the distance.

'That's rain, that's what it looks like from far away, like the clouds are kind of like, well, like this here cheese all dripping and drooping over the world... and that, over there, that's the blue sky, when nothing in it stops you seeing right up, and for some reason, though space is black, it's blue, like there's a sea up there, but I know there ain't. How you both doing in there anyway? You comfy?'

'We're fine,' said Alex through the fixed lips of Benny the bear.

The little bear's head tilted to one side.

'Just fine,' said Boudicca.

Animals Attack: Parts I to IV

It started with the cats and dogs. Just a handful of attacks at first, sporadic, spread out over several days and continents. It took a while before the connection was made. An old dear in Glasgow, chewed on by her cats while she slept. Two days later, a Mongolian farmer was set upon by his working pack of Tibetan mastiffs while he tended to his herd. But the news really struck when an American actress lost the best part of her brand new nose to a prize poodle she cradled in her arms, walking down Hollywood Boulevard while photographers snapped, and so did the dog.

News loves a connection, even a coincidence. The preposterous notion that these attacks, which continued to grow in number and severity, could be tangibly linked was held as absurd for at least a fortnight, but it didn't stop the mainstream taking the opportunity to mock the theorists.

'We believe that the animals are being activated, as it were, by fluctuations in the morphic field,' said the awkward-looking bearded man, made all the more awkward by the smooth, curved, primary-coloured television studio he had been installed into.

'Let me get this right,' came back the slickly gelled, high-cheek boned presenter, sporting his usual flick of mature grey hair tracing a line over his right ear, 'you think that these animal attacks, spread over the world, are connected by some kind of *energy* field, and that the animals are communicating and coordinating with each other?' If it had been acceptable for news presenters to stick their tongues below their bottom lips and make retarded sounds, he surely would have added this gesture.

'No, not quite. It's not really the animals communicating with each other. It's the planet communicating with the animals. We've seen it before with the mass suicides of fish and birds, amongst other animals. Those were the warning signs that a rebalance is coming, and this, this may be the means by which it happens.'

Of course the awkward bearded man and his associates were largely ignored at the time because, so far, no one had died. The old Glaswegian was badly bitten and was missing a good portion of her face when she woke up, the Mongolian farmer escaped by firing his gun and scattering the pack, and the actress needed little more than to repurchase the piece of plastic she had lost to the poodle. The other local, less noteworthy cases ran along the same lines, near misses and lucky escapes. It was only when people began dying that the tone changed.

It started with a breaking news story, or rather, it started and then the news story broke. It's sometimes hard to remember which comes first.

"Dozens of New Delhi homeless killed by stray dogs in overnight attacks."

It had taken a while for people to notice. The commuters were not unused to the sight of sleeping bodies beside the tracks, feet and heads poking out of the dirty sheets and torn sleeping bags, makeshift tents and broken rickshaw hammocks. Usually, however, the feet and heads were connected to the bodies; it was only when one train slowed for the signal that the left flank of the Indian Express got an eyeful of the carnage. The camps looked like the streets after Holi, but the only tone was red Hibiscus.

This atrocity alone would not have been enough. Stray dogs in Delhi are nothing unusual. A pack of rabid hounds in one locality does not an apocalypse make, and various naturalists and scientists were lined up that day to reassure the viewing public around the world that this sort of thing can happen. It is unusual, but it can, and obviously does, happen. Any notion of this being at all connected to the recent spate of attacks in other parts of the world were just coincidence, and nothing to worry about.

But then there was another story, stubbornly refusing to wait a decent amount of time since the last one in order to let the journalists and editors get their heads around it. This time it was the stray cats in Benidorm that had descended on a handful of flats through the open balconies of the Hotel Dynastic and driven several members of several families, spanning several nationalities, to jump from the fifteenth floor in blind panic, covered in slashing and biting felines. A few people avoided the balcony but were overwhelmed before they could get out. Many of the Spanish police who witnessed the scene said that those who didn't make it to the balcony were the unlucky ones.

From the swimming pool below, staff and tourists scattered to avoid the falling, most of whom found themselves facing a microphone before they could face up to their trauma:

'It was like a swarm, you know?' offered José, an attendant from the hotel. 'They came from the roof, they came up the fire escapes. Lots fell on the way, they didn't seem to care, like they were wild. I've not seen anything like this before. It is scary. They all went to the same floor. They passed other balconies and just poured into this one floor. This is not normal. I will be locking my windows, yes. And the people, they fell. You couldn't see them really, it was like a ¿*cuál es la palabra*? Coat? A coat, made of *gatos*, cats, all over them.'

It was soon speculated on websites that the floor the cats targeted housed the most diverse tourists in the building. English, German, Dutch, French, Italian and a few Spanish staff who lived onsite. The theory was that this was intended to 'send a message' across the world press, that the deaths of homeless Indians was not enough to get our attention, and we needed Western faces to fall before we would take any notice. They were at least right about that part. Within an hour, Delhi had moved down the pages and the cats of Benidorm had taken the lead while analysts had fingers on keys, tentatively exploring the possible links between the two. Feverously trying to find something that could fit into someone's respectable, empirical paradigm so they could get some meaningful commentary from somewhere. The inevitable came up first.

'Some have suggested that this could be linked to terrorism?' speculated one anchor, safe in his studio on video link up to Madrid's leading animal behaviourist.

'Terrorists? You think people did this? You see animals attacking humans, and you think people did this?' she replied with a refreshingly indignant tone. 'No way. They are doing this themselves. I don't know why.'

'But many other people in your field are saying that the only explanation could be human intervention, maybe a drug or gas that can alter behaviour. What would you say to that?'

'A drug that can make cats attack a specific floor of a building? That can make dogs choose the camp of the homeless next to tracks so that we all see it, when there are countless thousands of others they could have chosen? No, this is not drugs, this is something else.'

In typical media fashion, up against the fiery young specialist, also sitting comfortably and safe in the London studio, a stuffy fat white man with a lack of hair sat ready to respond with the voice of reason.

'Nonsense!' he interjected. 'These animals cannot and do not behave in this fashion under normal circumstances. Therefore the circumstances must not be normal. The only explanation for this has to be human intervention, accidental or intended. We'll probably find that there has been some kind of new compound fuel on the market that is poisoning water supplies, or something similar. To suggest anything else is absurd nonsense and frankly irresponsible.'

That night, Dr. Gideon George, after celebrating his fruitful afternoon of studio appearances and taking great delight in watching the several interviews he had appeared in over a large tumbler of good whisky, had his throat ripped out by his Cocker Spaniel, Sparky.

If there is one thing the news can't tolerate, it is too much news. That is when panic sets in. We want to see calm, collected, average-to-good-looking people reading out easily digestible reports with all the expert analysis we need to 'get it', without having to think for ourselves. At least, that is what they think we want, and conviction and resources combined can usually project your ideals onto others. When this tempered façade breaks down, so does this projection. We soon realise that we don't want experts speculating, we want experts to instruct us, to lead us, to help us. The attacks were becoming too numerous to report on with any semblance of authority and order. Bathers in Australia's Bunker Bay dragged to watery crimson graves by a school of great whites. Bears coming down from Mount Currie in British Columbia and attacking the towns. The animals of the Kruger National Park in South Africa at the compound fences, testing for weaknesses, lions and gazelles together, hunters and prey, side-by-side, with all eyes on us. This was no longer news, it was our lifeline. Tell us what we need to know. Should I kill my pets? Should I lock myself away? Is it happening everywhere? Tell us, help us, save us!

The answers didn't come. Contrary to the commonly held, Hollywood-fuelled belief, there was no emergency broadcast, no martial law. There were, however, underground bunkers, and that's where all those on the lists that had long been drawn up for broad emergencies found themselves. The fine line of trust we place in our leaders when handing over vast sums of our time and energy in producing resources wavered briefly as the crisis grew, and then snapped completely when it became apparent that they had gone away to somewhere safe. Or so they thought. The problem with underground bunkers is that they are underground, and underground isn't a particularly habitable place without light and energy. The burrowers saw to that. Electrical wiring isn't usually designed to withstand the teeth of moles, and the metal casings and brick structures are no match for determined ants, adept at finding and exploiting the tiniest of gaps, and gradually but surely prising them open with sheer force of numbers. When the lights went out, out came the rest of the insects through every cracked tile, every ventilation duct and loose pipe. It wasn't so much being eaten by insects, but drowning in them, or suffocating in the displaced earth they left in their wake. A few made it out, but not the senior officials who had been placed in the deepest and, they thought, most secure holes available. The ones who did escape kept their lives, but lost all authority with the first rays of sunshine that hit their faces. They were just like everyone else, left wondering what happens next. What to do about the animals.

Part II – The Stadium of Light

Of the huddled survivors, about as many who turned from God also turned to God. Many of the nurtured faithful who had never had to test the conviction of their belief, having had it spoon-fed to them from birth, soon found that hardship and terror were an easy replacement. For others, some who had never considered any path but the one they saw before them, could now feel the fire and brimstone for themselves. The fear compelled them, and in it they sought salvation. They pleaded and repented, they prayed and prostrated themselves before the nearest idol. It became both the rallying call and the dividing line for those who were left. While those groups who followed science would make dangerous sorties into the new world to capture animals for their experiments, others would build their borders strong, plant crops, read scripture and pray en masse for salvation.

Some communities emerged that achieved an uneasy balance of the two ideologies. One such place was the Stadium of Light. The docks of the Tyne and Wear had become quickly overwhelmed by those who thought taking to the sea was the only answer. The ships that left dock took more than they should carry but left behind many more, and as night fell, the dogs, cats and foxes came out. Left unchecked and feral, many were now rabid. Caught between the Tyne the Wear and the North Sea, the abandoned sought shelter and strong walls. The bright ones headed to the Stadium where they soon found the prudence of greedy football clubs keeping out the free-riders had paid off. Once the doors and gates were sealed, the mammals were kept at bay.

The bird attacks turned out to be a blessing after the initial nuisance. Pigeons and crows make a fairly decent meal, and it helps when your prey comes flying towards you at great speed (as long as you don't get caught in a flock). Water was close to hand, the Wear running just a little south of the Stadium. The pitch was turned over to crops salvaged from the nearest allotments. The shops outside were dangerous places to visit. It was always night in the shops, and what little could be brought safely back was temporary and soon consumed. The many conference rooms and bars became cantinas, hospitals and sheltered accommodation for those who most needed it. The majority of others sheltered in the stands, constructing makeshift huts from ripped-out seats and whatever materials they could find or salvage from outside. The Stadium became a shanty town, huddled around a central farm, surrounded on each side by ramshackle but operational amenities. The many glass-fronted executive suites were mostly given over to religion and science. Most denominations were represented, though many shared where ritual and practice did not interfere with each other's doctrines. The boxes that ran across the north-east side became known as 'God Alley', and opposite, where the amateur scientists set up shop was simply 'The Labs'. A handful of the remaining boxes that ran across the shorter concourses were allocated for education and entertainment.

These things did not happen naturally, however: a democracy of sorts was soon established after the chaos of the early months. It took a strong voice, much bolstered by the PA system, which at that time was still working. A fight had broken out amongst a new group that had joined and were wanting a share of the stockpiles. At first there were only about two hundred survivors who had become comfortable with each other's company, united against the threat of the outside world. So when another hundred arrived, fresh from abandoning the Sunderland University campus (which had become overrun from the breeding grounds of the surrounding parks), the division of aid and food became critical. The original settlers had figured out how to hunt the birds, and when the self-appointed leader of the new group had asked for food from the tinned stockpile, he was refused and told instead to walk out to the centre of the pitch with a frying pan, and wait.

The young man, an undergraduate psychologist who had skilfully employed his study to the dynamic of group survival, did not argue. He took the dented frying pan, streaked with a metallic red, from the alpha survivors and walked out. His group and the originals watched from the shelter of the stands. At this time the pitch was overgrown, they had not yet figured out the bounty of this resource, and no crops had been sown. The student stood on what he guessed was roughly the centre spot and waited. Nothing happened. He looked up and around, wondering what it was he was meant to do. He searched his memory and reasoning to try and figure out why they had asked him to do something so bizarre when all he wanted was food, and then he saw it. A speck in the sky was heading towards him. Now it was a line, now it was a ball with two curved shapes on each side. He was unused to bird attacks, having lived in shelter where possible, but he had seen from his campus windows the damage they could cause. They may not kill you, but being blinded in a world of savage animals was certainly not much of a consolation.

He went to run, but the others called out, 'Kill it!' so he stood his ground, and the frying pan melted into context in his mind. He had never been any good at hitting things before. He was a hopeless sportsman who used to feebly wave his rounders bat at school and run to first base in full knowledge that he had never, and would never, make contact. And here he was, pan in hand, about to take out a crow? A pigeon? A buzzard? It got bigger and bigger as it approached; it was still some way off but its form had focussed into a hunchbacked torpedo, cutting through the air, wings tucked back on a steep descent. It was an eagle, a golden eagle, he guessed, by its size and shimmer, and it was nearly upon him. He swung back the pan, it was his only option now, he waited a second, a second in which his mind tried to judge the speed, distance and time before the great bird would collide with him. He brought the pan around in an arch, not thinking to sidestep and use the velocity of the animal against it or simply cover his face with the pan. Instead, he treated it like a baseball, and as he missed his home run and his body turned with the inertia of his failed swing, the eagle crashed into the side of his head, killing him, and the bird, instantly.

It was then that the fight broke out. The two groups who had stood side-by-side as they watched the young man's death unfold, first screamed then gasped, then turned. It was the new group who fought with more vigour. They had followed the student - Mark was his name, had they not even asked? Why would they do such a thing? The original group tried to explain that it was usually small birds, crows and the like, that they wanted him to learn how to hunt: why didn't he move? How were they supposed to know? How many eagles can there be in England? People tumbled over seats and down sharp stairways as they wrestled, kicked and punched. The stands were once more alive with the sound of angry shouts and violence, until a voice broke through, echoing over the desperate rage.

'Stop! Stop! What are you doing?'

The people stopped and turned instinctively. None of them knew where the microphone for the tannoy was, so all they could do was stand.

'We *need* rules. We *need* to communicate. Or we'll all be dead. Haven't enough people died at the teeth and claws of the animals already? Are there not enough bodies floating down the Tyne that we need to add some more? Stop, for the love of God or of simple reason, just stop! I'm coming down. We need to talk.'

And so it was that Leticia Coveney became the first voice to speak above the others, the first to plead for reason, the first to take votes and to draw up rotas. The first leader who, by the only virtue of suggesting order, was appointed to keep it.

Part III – A summary of 'The Rules of the Stadium of Light', as drafted by Leticia Coveney and committee and voted into Constitution by the survivors therein.

Note: These rules are written in plain English as much as possible. Those here who have some law have by their own admission decided this is no place for their language and learning, based it as was upon structures now destroyed and defunct. Those who have some philosophy, as myself, have retreated to basics, to build new foundations for our community based on the new paradigm we find ourselves in. We will endeavour to base our rules on sound thinking and reason, on need and utility, for it is only with careful calculation and moral foundations that we will survive and remain part of whatever this world becomes. – Leticia Coveney

The rules were clear, robust and covered almost all aspects of life in the Stadium. Roles were devised, voted for and awarded on a rotational basis that allowed re-election for those who performed the duty well. All shares of basic food and provisions were to be equal, any extra demand distributed on a needs basis. Everyone not engaged in critical tasks due to specialisms or those unable due to medical conditions were rotated on agricultural, construction, defence and reconnaissance duties, although those who were highly skilled and willing in the more dangerous tasks were able to distribute their duties more freely.

A great emphasis was placed on skill-sharing. A core of able gatherers and hunters soon emerged, charged with leaving the Stadium to find supplies and hunt food. They were required, when possible, to bring along a quota of the less skilled so that more would gain the experience needed. The same went for medical, agricultural and construction tasks, which were usually the more sought-after training opportunities, posing less risk to one's life.

No elected positions lasted more than a month without a vote. There was already little else to do outside of basic survival, so the demographics were hardly apathetic. Voting became an actively debated and discussed activity, and no boundaries existed between the representatives and the rest of the group. There was no special arrangement for those in charge, other than the use of an office during the day. At night, all slept in the shelters and huddled for warmth.

There were several major positions to emerge from the rules. The most senior was the chairperson, appointed to call to order the thirteen-strong elect group of representatives and have final say in deadlock situations and the ability to set priority of agenda items. In theory, all roles answered to the chairperson, though it was always the majority will of the representatives that prevailed.

The chief medical officer, unlike the chairperson which rotated fairly often, was not open to vote and was instead based on expertise. Luckily for this group, unlike so many others that perished, a doctor by the name of Amir Shamsi was one of the original survivors to arrive at the Stadium. He conceived and organised his own activities and only a motion forwarded by the chairperson and unanimously upheld by all elected representatives could ever contradict or dismiss him. The CMO had final say in all matters of health and hygiene, the power to remove people from duties, and the power to relieve role-holders on grounds of diminished responsibility or health concerns. Mainly, however, his time was spent relentlessly fighting the plethora of ailments and injuries that befell the group, with little equipment or medicine.

The Quartermaster was in charge of all distribution of supplies and drew up lists of provisions needed, based on reports from the other divisions. It was the Quartermaster's job to ensure all had basic food, clothing and materials with which to build and maintain shelter. They held the keys to the stores and the inventories, had final say on who got what and when, and were only able to be overturned by a majority committee vote if concerns were raised by the chairperson or the CMO. In this way, despite the efforts of the first few candidates to abuse this position, an uneasy balance was eventually achieved. The Quartermaster's role was not a popular one, and took selflessness to perform.

The guard leader was responsible for the security of the Stadium and organising reconnaissance, and, although an elected role, a grace period was initially awarded to an Army officer amongst the group who was tasked with setting up the guard rotation, training, equipment and defences as a priority. Her name was Darleen Reynolds and she didn't make it to the first vote. She got caught in the rigging for the weight drops she had designed to smash down on any persistent animals at the walls. She didn't die on impact when she fell to the ground: she fell into a pack. Nothing remained when the beasts finally cleared. The guard leader then became a voted role, no one person having a greater discernible aptitude than the next to finish her preparatory work. From that point on, it was improvisation and collaboration amongst the untrained. There was a lot of crossover between the guard volunteers and the gatherers. This became of some concern as it was the guards who were also responsible for maintaining order within the camp, being the only ones authorised to use restraint or violence if needed (under very strict conditions set by the committee). A subgroup, a militia almost, was feared to be rising. An uneasy balance emerged when one man, Adrian Layton, was consistently voted guard leader month after month thanks to the support of his men and a core of survivors who happily accepted the extra provisions he smuggled past the Quartermaster.

The crops that were eventually sown in the centre field, and in any other space made available in the Stadium (certain executive boxes made for good greenhouses), were coordinated by the head gardener. This role was casually elected amongst those with the best credentials who agreed a rotational basis between them. All in all, five agricultural leaders emerged, each of whom took responsibility for various crops and coordinated chores. It was a constant battle and took almost as much improvisation as the guard leader to think around the practicality of limited topsoil, limited light and the best crops to grow from the little that could be salvaged.

Other roles of less power and varying importance included the catering manager, the scientific researchers, the theologians (a selection of faiths nominated representatives if no ordained members were in the group), the construction pool coordinator (who reported to the Quartermaster), and even an entertainments manager. Teachers were taken from volunteers and lessons were strictly limited to practical and survival skills as a priority. Children and adults alike attended classes.

Many tried, and failed, to create roles that were not set out in Leticia's constitution. 'Relics of the old world,' she called them. Communication officers, moral officers, think-tank coordinators, all reared their heads and tried to use their self-appointed titles to justify shirking daily activities. They were not tolerated. Any tasks that had merit were added to existing roles. Some unofficial roles, especially those of apprentice, came up and were allowed, but not at the expense of fair contribution to the wider group needs. Never at that cost.

Leticia held a few roles in the early months, and commanded popularity. She balanced this by not standing for election for the same role on more than one consecutive occasion, all too aware that as the author of the constitution, she was best poised to bastardise it. Whether she intended to or not, that temptation and pressure would always be present.

The constitution itself spanned a hundred A4 pages, carefully handwritten by Leticia herself initially, with any amendments and additions carefully version-logged and filed, and securely held for reference. Abridged, digestible versions were hand-copied and distributed. Group meetings were held to cover the main points. People were happy to have them, and for a while they created a life for themselves, all be it hard and beset with danger. People died, but more lived. New survivors to the camp were integrated for a time, until one day, the first major constitutional amendment had to be made.

Part IV - There's more at the door

'Gentlemen, ladies, what can I do for you?' asked Leticia as she scanned the mostly familiar faces of the assembled committee, gathered around the boardroom table.

Acting chairperson David White sat down first, prompting all but Adrian Layton to do the same. Adrian remained standing as he was, slightly to the left of his chair, arms folded, legs wide.

'Have mine if you like,' he gestured to his empty seat. There were no others. Chairs made good firewood, so exactly thirteen remained in the boardroom for the committee members.

'I'm okay. Just what is this about? I've got...' She limply thumb-signalled over her shoulder to a task she guessed was now on hold.

'We're full,' said the chairman. All eyes watched Leticia who responded quickly to see off her rapidly tensing shoulders and mood.

'Look, we have this every month. I understand, but it's just not true. There's still space, you can see for yourselves. Do we have to have this again?' She eyed the statue that was Adrian Layton, expecting his usual protectionist gibber.

'Yes we do this time, Leticia. Please. Sit down,' said Doctor Shamsi.

Leticia sat down. The doctor had spoken.

***

Constitutional Amendment #15:

"If such a time arrives, as agreed by the unanimous vote of the residing committee members, that the Stadium can no longer support the arrival of new survivors without seriously jeopardising the safety and well-being of the incumbent population, a no-exception policy of refusal for shelter will be adopted. This will remain in place until a further unanimous vote overturns the decision.

Guidance for contact with non-resident survivors:

Non-resident survivor groups who approach the Stadium should not be communicated with unless by their actions they threaten the perimeter security. In such a case, a verbal warning should be issued with a strict compliance time of no more than five minutes. If this is not adhered to, a warning shot can be fired to encourage compliance. If, following this they persist, the guard is permitted to use whatever force necessary to encourage dispersal, or if that is not possible, eliminate the threat to our people.

Non-resident survivors encountered outside the stadium during reconnaissance missions should also be avoided at all costs, and every effort made to prevent them learning of our settlement. If contact is impossible to avoid, a suitable cover story for the group should be used to encourage them to depart. This will be coordinated with the guard leader before every mission. In extreme circumstances, as always, the use of force is permitted if no alternative exists, as decided by the expedition leader.

No bartering for skills or resources is to ever take place and is an expellable offence."

The last point of the amendment was hotly contested at the time of its conception.

'Well why the hell would we wanna do that?' barked Layton. 'What if the guy's a commando or, I dunno, a surgeon? Or packing guns, yeah?'

'What if he, or she, isn't?' Leticia stared at him unblinking. 'What if they just want to get in? And anyway, where do we draw the line? You want to chuck someone else out to let them in? You want to start deciding who deserves to stay and who doesn't? It's you who wanted this all along. Live with it. You want lockdown. You got it. But it has to be airtight, do you understand?'

He didn't understand, but the motion was passed and the constitution amended. It took a few weeks before the amendment was to be tested.

***

It was a rookie guard who first spotted the boat from the south stand watch.

'It's coming from the east,' he whispered into his walkie-talkie, as if the people on-board could hear him.

'Stay covered, but keep eyes on it. Hopefully it'll pass. What kind of boat?' crackled Layton through the speaker.

'It's the ferry, sir, the Shields ferry.'

The boat didn't pass, it stopped and anchored just past the high embankments north of the Stadium. It was difficult for the guard to see what was happening. They just had to wait. No contingency was needed, despite the amalgam of apparatus and pulley systems hanging from the framework against the skyline. There was no point trying to make the place look like it had never been occupied: that would only encourage them and they just needed to stay out of sight. The doors and gates were tightly sealed. It would take effort to gain access even if they bothered trying, but with the last hour of light or so from an October afternoon, no one would be hanging around long. The foxes would see to that.

Either way, the welcoming committee moved into place by the main doors as they always did with new arrivals, but this time they kept out of sight, and the plan dictated they weren't to be so welcoming.

The chairman, Leticia, Dr. Shamsi and Adrian waited in the entrance behind the reinforcements. Only a small crawl hole allowed them out from below the barricade, through a smashed panel and out to the perimeter fence, the iron guard, bent and bloodied by persistent attack, but still holding strong. Generally, none of the usual entrances were used for anything but meet and greet, and it took several layers of reinforcements to get through. Outside, further sandbags and debris formed another layer of defence at the bottom of the steps, some yards away from the fans' monument depicting a family reaching together to the frame of a hollow globe, within which was sprawled the skeleton of a Rottweiler, the remnants of a bludgeoned trophy kill discarded by an overzealous survivor in the days before the constitution.

From the safety of the barricade, the committee gathered around the peephole as they heard several sets of footsteps approaching. A group emerged, unaware of their spectators. Seven or eight people at least, spiralling slowly with their backs to each other, a few armed with handguns, most with pipes or nailed sticks. They looked like your typical small wandering group, surviving from one hole to the next until too many animals caught their scent and they had to move on. Leticia and the others could hear them talking, but couldn't yet see them clearly. Two voices seemed to rise above the others.

'Okay. Obviously someone's been here, or is here,' said a male voice with a mature rasp and gravel.

'We should go in,' answered another male, sharp and quick, agitated. The kind of voice you don't want to hear from someone holding a gun.

'It's probably booby-trapped,' said the first. 'If they are here, they know we are.'

Leticia liked the sound of that voice. It was calm, collected, thinking, comforting. The other, however, made her worried. Very worried.

'Go on then!' the panicked man shouted. 'If you're here, say something! Go on! We need help!'

Through the hole they could now see the nervous fellow more clearly. All the time he was asking for help he was clutching his gun and waving it from place to place, looking for signs of movement. Adrian shot side eyes to Leticia and the others as he slowly reached for his holster. Leticia reached over with one hand and grabbed his wrist. She slowly shook her head. Adrian signalled with his free hand the universal 'it's alright' wave, and Leticia allowed him to unclip and remove his gun. He mouthed a 'just in case' to her and she understood. They watched.

Outside a similar scene was happening.

'Put it down, Mike,' said the first voice.

'What? But, wh-what if they...?'

'Put it down, Mike,' the voice repeated slower, calmer, yet somehow more aggressive by its metre.

They saw the flinching man lower his arms. They couldn't see faces, just torsos clad in the usual bizarre combinations. Most people in this world looked like they had just raided an Army surplus store and a charity shop. One of the torsos, clad in a green woodcutter shirt beneath a deep blue reefer jacket, stepped forward. It belonged to the voice of reason.

'If anyone is here, and you can hear me, my name is Vaughn. These are my friends. There are seven of us here and another five on our boat. We thought we were safe offshore. We were wrong and we need help. We need somewhere on land to recuperate, to heal.'

Leticia twitched with an impossible feeling. She pushed her head into the spyhole. Adrian clutched her shoulder and tried to pull her back. The doctor and chairman were knocked back from their awkward crouches and tumbled. A foot hit a loose crate stacked beside them; it dislodged, and the stack creaked as it found a new equilibrium. Footsteps from outside shuffled together as the group heard.

'They are in there, man, I told you. Come out! Go on! We're not beasts, let us in!' shouted the impetuous voice of Mike.

'Hold it, hold it!' pleaded Vaughn.

'Is that you?' shouted Leticia, unthinking, her voice croaking in her throat.

Everyone stopped. Adrian managed to pull Leticia out from the hole and fix her in his glare.

'What the hell are you doing? You forgotten your own rules?'

'I know him,' she said. Puddles formed and clung to her lashes. 'It's my dad.'

Adrian pulled back and let her go. Leticia stood up on a crate and looked over the barriers. She could just about see. The group outside could only make out black hair falling over her dark forehead, and half-moon eyes above the sandbags.

'Hello,' called Vaughn Coveney at the appearance of what he could just about fathom was a girl. 'My name's Vaughn, these are my friends…'

'I heard you the first time,' shouted Leticia. She used her old 'phone voice' from the days before the creatures, to hide her accent.

'Then you know we need help?' called her father.

'There's no help to be had here. There's no room. Please go.'

'We don't want to stay. We just need somewhere to rest up. We have provisions. We can trade, be useful.'

Leticia bowed her head and bit her lip. In doing so she saw the committee still crouched below her, all three, just looking at her like befuddled children. Even Adrian's eyes seemed to be saying, 'This is different, it's okay'. But she knew this wasn't different. How had she forgotten it? Family! It had been so long since anyone had found someone they'd lost that it hadn't occurred to her, or anyone else. What if the enemy at the gate was family? What happens then? But it wasn't just her dad. It was her dad and at least a dozen others. Once they were in, they wouldn't be leaving. And what then? The doctor had told her in no uncertain terms, that's it: any more and we start dying. The Quartermaster couldn't meet demand. More and more people were coming back from sorties with injuries that needed tending. It was either expel the weak or accept the strangers. What kind of a choice is that?

'Leticia,' called up the doctor in a strained whisper, 'we can make an exception.'

'For all of them?' she asked, and swallowed hard. The doctor didn't answer. 'I thought not.'

'Then you go,' said Adrian.

Leticia's pupils sank to the bottom of her sockets as she went deep inside. She had no inner voice, just a blank and uneasy feeling. She was waiting on it to mean something, then there was a crack.

The shot rang out and was followed by the *'fumfff'* of a sandbag absorbing a bullet.

'Stop it! Put it down, man! You'll get us all killed!'

Leticia looked over to see her Father struggling with the anxious shooter. They both had their hands on the gun, but Mike had the stronger grip. The other people in the group backed off and dodged as the two men swung around, the barrel zigzagging a line across all their fates.

'Dad!' cried Leticia from somewhere within, somewhere unasked for.

Vaughn looked up, giving his adversary just enough time to throw him off and aim the gun straight at Leticia's face. Another crack rang out. Mike fell dead as a bullet ripped through his eye.

Adrian hopped down from where he had pulled himself onto the barrier. He kept his gun raised as he approached the dead man. He had never shot a man before, but this one, he reconciled, was as bad as the animals. The rest of the group fell into a huddle around Vaughn who held up his hands on their behalf. Leticia stood shaking from her vantage point. The doctor and the chairman pulled themselves up but stayed behind cover while trying to coax her down.

'He didn't speak for us,' said Vaughn to the contorted face of Adrian who was breathing hard and approaching fast. 'We understand. You did what you needed to do.'

'Get inside,' Adrian snarled, his gun pointed at the group.

'It's okay.' Vaughn lowered his hands. 'We'll go. We'll just turn and go. Leticia!' he shouted, keeping his eyes fixed on Adrian, 'if you want to come with us, that's fine. But it's got to be now.'

'Get inside! Now!'

Vaughn registered a shift in Adrian's stare, over his shoulder to the thistle and dock jungle of the former car park behind them. He steadily turned his head and caught the same rustle approaching. He signalled to his people: they crouched and passed Adrian on each side, moving quickly towards the barricade, leaving Adrian, gun pointed into the leafy unknown.

The lions came. One fell with Adrian's first bullet, the others recoiled with the gun and then pounced. Three of the great beasts, two males and a female, a blur of sandy manes matted with foam and blood, piled into Adrian. Jaws flashed before his eyes, no lifetime, just tooth and claw.

Vaughn and the others piled over the barricades while the lions were busy with their kill. They were helped up and over by the doctor, the chairman and Leticia, who had broken her trance when Adrian fell. She always thought it would be pride that killed him: she was almost right.

Safely inside the stadium, back behind the steel and barbed gates, Leticia embraced her father while the rest panted, crouched and collapsed around the foyer. Vaughn broke the embrace and held his little girl at arm's length to get a good look at her.

'I can't believe I found you. I thought...'

'So did I.'

The chairman awkwardly stood by them while the doctor attended to the others.

'I'm sorry to interrupt this happy reunion, but what now, Leticia? What next? We've got hundreds already, and this group isn't going to be the last to find us. I don't want to turn any more away, it's just not going to happen without trouble. No offence,' he added, with a tiny nod to Vaughn.

'I don't know. Another settlement maybe? The lab rats are close to getting the radios working. Just a few more parts, they say. The constitution works here, it can work somewhere else.'

'We were heading somewhere,' Vaughn interjected, 'before we had to stop here. It was a crazy idea, but we think it might work. We needed to get up the water, but we can make it, I think. What's this constitution?'

'Your daughter,' said the chairman, 'gave us a model to work to, a way to work together. She thought of everything - well, nearly everything. But if we can get it out to other locations, if we can coordinate, we might just get this world back. At least some of it.'

'You did that, honey?'

'Yeah. I did. But I forgot,' her voice cracked. 'I forgot about family.'

Vaughn brought her close and hugged her tight.

'You kept hundreds of people alive and showed them how to survive together and you think you forgot family?' he said, muzzling his head into her hair. 'No, honey. You didn't forget.'

Leticia pulled herself away and wiped her cheeks with the palms of her hands. Her dad smiled as he watched her compose herself. She was strong. He always knew she was.

'So,' said Leticia, hands on hips, sharp and ready. 'Where were you heading?'

'The zoo, honey, we're going to the zoo,' said Vaughn.

The Next Level

As Gerry came round, the slow drip, drip, drip of nearby water was his sole sensation. All else was dark, quiet. Soon he realised he was uncomfortable, contorted somehow, but this feeling was left unexplored with the sound of a heavy door opening.

'Hello? Who's there?' said Gerry, who, in trying to move, found the source of his discomfort. His hands and legs were bound together behind him and attached to a chair he could now tell he was sitting on. The chair clattered slightly with his awkward attempts at movement. Gerry soon stopped, feeling the tilt of the front legs and quite unable to loosen his hands: the idea of a face full of floor kept him still.

The door creaked to a halt, yet no light had accompanied its opening. A palatable silence of company in the dark place took over.

'Where am I? Where is this place?' Gerry asked the void.

'There's no use trying to get free. I'm good with knots,' replied a voice from unseen lips somewhere before him. The voice was educated, British, devoid of discernible accent, like a Pathé newsreel.

'Let me go!' protested Gerry, this time struggling only with his wrists and hands. He grunted as the binds tightened in response.

'We'll talk later. When you've calmed down,' said the voice. The door closed. The drip, drip, drip grew to fill the silence and Gerry fell into an uneasy sleep.

***

When he awoke, nothing had changed. At least, as far as he could tell from his orientation to the dark relentless dripping. He tried to clear his mind, but it was a dense fog. Survival was the only light that could shine through it.

'Hello? I'm ready to talk. If that's what you want. Hell...' Gerry's shouts were cut short by the opening of the door. He steadied his breathing, moderated his tone.

'I'm ready to talk,'

'Are you calm?' asked the same voice.

'Yes. Perfectly. Wh - what do you want to talk about?'

'Liar!' shouted the voice, with a depth of malice.

The door closed again.

***

'Wake up. Wakey-wakey.'

The shock of the water against his face was how Gerry knew he had even been sleeping again. He seemed to be drifting to and fro, unable to tell if it was the darkness of his eyes or the room before him. He gasped with the sensation: he tilted backwards and narrowly avoided falling.

'What? Where am I?' he asked, experiencing his first confusion all over again.

'Don't worry, your eyes are open. It's just very dark in here. Now, are you ready to talk?' asked the voice, and with it, Gerry's loose memories of his earlier encounter returned.

'Yes. I'm ready.'

'Good. And are you calm?'

'No, not really,' replied Gerry.

'Even better! It would be unreasonable to expect you to be calm when you're tied to a chair in a dark room. Don't you think?'

'Yes.'

'So why did you say you were calm when I asked before?'

'I, I don't know. I thought that's what you wanted.'

'Whoever goes tying people to chairs in dark rooms and wants them to be calm? That doesn't make any sense, does it?'

The voice was leading him, inflecting and directing his answers like a primary schoolteacher trying to impress the error of his ways.

'I suppose not.'

'Apologise.' The voice had returned to its guttural form.

'I'm sorry,' Gerry muttered.

'Well done!' The voice jumped back to jovial teacher. 'We're making progress. You're on the first step to your rehabilitation.'

'My what?'

'Your rehabilitation.'

'But, I haven't done anything.' Despite his vague memory, Gerry couldn't recall any rattling of skeletons in closets or otherwise.

'Haven't you? We'll see about that.'

'Are you a terrorist?' asked Gerry, starting to compose his thoughts. The voice laughed loud and hard.

'Are you terrified?'

Gerry searched for prudence in his response but was interrupted by the return of the gravelly, demon tones.

'Are you terrified?!' demanded the voice.

'Yes!' screamed Gerry, honestly.

Again the voice bounced back to calm.

'Well, then I must be. By your reckoning, anyway.'

'How did I get here? I can't remember.'

'That's not important. What's important is are you ever going to get out?'

'What do you want? If it's money, they won't pay. They won't negotiate.'

'That's rather a shame. Oh well.'

Once again the door closed.

'No! Come back!' pleaded Gerry. But he was alone.

***

'Hello.'

The new voice called out, without the usual accompaniment of the creaking door, as if the voice's owner had been in the room the whole time. It was the voice of a girl, Gerry thought, a young girl. He answered softly.

'Hello? Who's that?'

'I'm not meant to say,' said the girl. Gerry found it hard to pinpoint where from.

'That's okay. Is your daddy here?'

'He's not my daddy!' the little girl giggled.

'The man who was here before, is he here?'

'No. It's just me.'

Gerry heard some clanging and scuffles, as if from above him. The little girl's voice seemed to be coming from the same direction.

'Can you tell me who the man is? If he's not your daddy.'

'He's my uncle,' she said, succinctly.

'What's his name?'

'He's just my uncle. He's everybody's uncle.'

This was it. The appearance of the little girl made him believe that beyond the dark room there was probably a house and a family of some kind, which meant there would be transport, places to hide and run, a chance. She probably wasn't meant to be here. He had to act quickly.

'I see. Listen, are you good at knots? I bet you are, eh?'

'I'm not going to let you go. I know what you did. It's very bad.'

The girl sounded as if she were telling off a doll, mimicking her own chastisement.

'And what did I do? Go on, tell me. I've forgotten.'

Maybe escape wasn't an option, thought Gerry, but information is just as important.

'No you haven't. You're lying.'

'Again,' said the voice of the unseen man with the BBC accent. If Gerry had anywhere to jump to, he would have done so at the unexpected interjection. His anger rose as it does following a slap in the face, a stubbed toe, an unfair affront to the senses.

'Jesus! So you *are* here? I demand you let me go. They'll come looking for me, you know. Ministers don't just disappear. You have no idea what you've done, what you're in for.'

'Could you leave us alone a moment, sweetheart?' the voice said softly.

'Yes, Uncle,' replied the little girl.

There was a scampering above Gerry, the sound of hatches or latches or something metallic and moveable.

'I have every idea what I've done. It was, after all, my idea,' said the voice he now knew as 'Uncle'.

'When they find me...'

'That's really besides the point. Yes, I suppose they probably will find you. But it's the manner in which you are found which is the important thing.'

The voice seemed to be getting closer, circling him. It helped Gerry to realise that he must be in the centre of the room, with enough space for someone to circumnavigate his position. More information. Keep him talking, Gerry thought, find out more.

'What do you mean?'

'I mean, how many bits of you there are to find is probably more important to you at this present moment than anything else.'

'Are you going to kill me?'

The question had been building, and he hadn't dared ask it before, in fear of the answer, but it now seemed as appropriate a time as any, given the mention of body parts.

'Yes. Eventually. How does that make you feel?'

It made him feel several things. His bowels shifted uneasily, his stomach lifted and dropped, his head swam, his eyes filled.

'Oh God, oh God. Please. Please no. I'll do anything. Please,' sobbed Gerry. He was no longer in control of his strategy.

'Anything?'

'Whatever you want, just don't kill me.'

He could feel the tears run down his face. It was a feeling he hadn't experienced for a long time. He remembered the sting that salt water leaves on your skin after weeping and wiping your face dry over and over. It was an old, dusty memory.

'That's interesting. I'll have to think about it. How about some music while you wait?' asked the voice, but the door closed before Gerry could answer, and the music started.

'Things, can only get better. Can only get better...' echoed around him, and did not stop for a length of time Gerry could only calculate as 'torturous'.

***

A machine clicked. The music stopped. Gerry snapped out of the waking sleep he had fallen into as a defence against hours of the same song on repeat, that mocking song which he never wanted to hear again.

'I don't like that song.'

It was the little girl. Gerry pulled himself up in the chair as best he could.

'Oh thank you, thank God,' said Gerry.

'Do you believe in God?' asked the little girl.

'Yes.'

'You didn't used to, though. Uncle says you only started believing in God when you became important,' said the little girl, who by now, Gerry had decided, held little hope for salvation. If her voice had not been so distinctive, he could almost believe the girl and this 'Uncle' were one and the same person.

'No, I always believed. I just didn't used to go to church.'

A growing fear of religious undertones was building in Gerry. Money, politics, he could deal with; fundamentalists were a different breed.

'But do you *really* believe? Or are you just going because you think you should?' the girl quizzed.

'Why are you asking me this? Is your uncle here? Are you? Why are you having her ask me this? Can't you do your own dirty work?' Gerry shouted while looking around the chamber - not that he could see. No matter how much time had passed, his eyes had nothing to adjust to.

'Uncle isn't here this time. I'll undo your knots if you like?'

Suddenly the voice was right behind his left ear. She must have climbed down while he was shouting. He spoke gently to her.

'Yes, yes please. My wrists are very sore.'

'Okay.'

Gerry felt some pressure on the binds around his wrists, but it soon stopped.

'Oh wait. First I want you to answer my question,' said the girl, still close by and behind.

'I thought I had.'

'No you didn't, silly. I asked if you *really* believe in God.'

'Yes I do. Like I said.'

'I don't believe you. I'm not going to untie you if I don't believe you.'

Gerry heard what he imagined to be the stamp of a tiny, petulant foot. Time to try something else.

'Alright, alright, I don't believe in God. I just go to church because I'm expected to. Now will you untie me?

'But that's lying. You shouldn't say you believe in God if you don't really. No one would mind,' said the voice that seemed to be growing distant again.

'Yes you're right,' Gerry said desperately, 'it was very bad of me, now please, my wrists.'

'I don't know now. You lied.'

'I only did it so I could help people.'

'How does lying about God help people?'

The voice was definitely back up in the roof, the rafters, whatever was up there.

'Well, some people, they won't vote for you or support you if they think you don't believe in God. And I, I want to help these people but I need their support.'

'So you lie to help people?' said the girl, almost convinced.

'It was a little white lie. You've heard of those, haven't you?'

'No.'

'It's when lying to someone is the best thing for them, even though they don't know it. When it does more good than harm, in the long run.'

Gerry felt momentum building. The girl was swaying to him, he could feel it.

'I think I understand. It's like me saying I was going to undo those knots. It will do you more good, in the long run.'

The girl laughed, a hatch closed. Gerry was alone again.

'No! No! Come back! No!'

***

The next time the door opened, Gerry was ready.

'So, it's about God, is it? Is this a cult?' he asked, not caring whether it was the girl or the uncle who had just entered the room. There was no answer, save the slamming of the door.

'I'll take that as a yes. You want me to repent? Is that it?'

He knew he was in company. He could hear breathing.

'Well, it's the one thing I can't do for you. You can't make me believe something I don't. And if I say I do, you won't believe me. Seems we're at an impasse here, wouldn't you say?

The breathing continued, but still no reply.

'What I can do for you, though, if you let me go, is protect you. Make sure no one comes knocking down doors when I'm found. Hell, you don't even have to let me know where I've been. Blindfold me and throw me out somewhere. Even if I was lying I wouldn't have much chance of finding you.'

The encouraging silence soon became disconcerting. The breathing became lighter, and phased as if enveloped by electronic filters. It spiralled around his ears.

'Come on, say something! Say something!' he shouted out.

'Gerry?' came the reply. A soft voice. A voice he knew from somewhere.

'Who's that?'

'Gerry, it's me,' said his wife.

'Emma? They've got you, too? Oh God. I'm so sorry.'

Gerry cried again, the tears lapping over the dried saline crystals from the last time.

'Why are you crying?' asked Emma.

'I don't know what they're going to do to us. They said they're going to kill me. I'm so sorry.'

'Why are you sorry? This is what you wanted,' she replied. Her voice was soft, as usual, but calm with it. Too calm.

'Are you hurt? Have they drugged you?' he asked, trying to look vaguely in the direction of his wife's voice.

'This is what you want, isn't it?' she continued, seemingly unaffected by the desperate cries of her captive husband.

'Why are you saying that? How did you get here?'

Emma's voice began to phase, just like the breathing had before she arrived. Like a guitar pedal on a psychedelic record.

'He's not making any sense. Are you sure this thing's safe?' Emma said, but it was fading.

'Who are you talking to?' Gerry asked his quickly diminishing wife. The response, however, came from the familiar voice of Uncle, but this, too, was distant, wobbly.

'One moment. You've phased through into the programme.'

With that, the voices spiralled away into nothing. The door opened.

'Where did she go? What have you done with her?' Gerry demanded of the visitor.

'With who?' said Uncle, but this time the voice was present in the room, solid and tangible.

'My wife! She was here!'

'There's nobody else here but you and me.'

'I just spoke to her, and she spoke back, and then there was a voice, your voice, only...' Gerry tailed off into his thoughts. Had he been asleep? It was so hard to tell.

'Oh dear,' the voice of Uncle picked up, 'the hallucinations are starting to kick in. It can happen spontaneously when people are kept in the dark for too long. They start to see things that aren't there. Fascinating condition, really, when you think about it. We have such active minds that in the absence of any stimuli they start to project outwards, just to keep us sane. Most people would think the hallucinations are insanity, but what would be more insane than an eternal void? Then again, I suppose you would disagree.'

'I can't take much more of this. You're trying to break me,' Gerry whimpered.

'Not at all!' said Uncle, rather spritely. 'You're already broken. We're trying to fix you.'

'We? Who's we? You and the little girl? Or are there more of you? Waiting for the next passing comet to take your souls into outer space or some nonsense? What do you need me for? Why don't you just get on with it and take your suicide pills. Transcend or whatever it is.'

'You think we're a cult?' said Uncle, surprised.

'Aren't you?'

'Depends. The definition of a cult, I expect, is a group of people dedicated to the worship of a divine being or beings, and characterised by extreme methods of worship. I mean, otherwise everyone would be in a cult, wouldn't they?'

'Unless you don't believe in a divine being,' said Gerry.

'But what is a divine being? Something with supernatural powers over nature and humanity? Can we agree on that, in a broad sense?'

The voice was less patronising. It felt to Gerry as if he had moved up from primary school to sixth-form college and was starting to get talked to like an adult. He cringed at the little flare of self-respect this brought him.

'What does it matter?'

'Well it should matter to you. That's what you are,' said Uncle.

'You think I'm a God?'

'Not when you're tied to this chair, in a dark room, no. But at times. Yes.'

'Why?'

'Well, because you do have a supernatural power over humanity and nature, don't you?

'There's nothing supernatural about my power,' said Gerry as he struggled to comprehend if they now wanted to worship or sacrifice him.

'Isn't there? You say the word and people live or die. That's rather extraordinary.'

Gerry recognised this rhetoric. He had heard similar arguments before from idealists who think you can run the world on hemp and solar power alone. His confidence grew as he entered his comfort zone. Maybe they were just students. Stupid, radical maybe, but students nonetheless, with jellied backbones, unformed and easily wavered. Still, to be careful, Gerry tried to moot his usual condescending tones when dealing with such people.

'It doesn't work like that! That's just scaremongering and excuses. I represent people, I make choices on behalf of people, for their own good. I don't just click my fingers and people die.'

'But people do die, when you make those choices, don't they? When you decide how much they are worth, what they are entitled to, what they're *not* entitled to.'

'That's not my intention. People would die anyway; *more* people would die without us.'

The voice of Uncle paused a moment before replying.

'Would less people die if someone else was making the choices?' it finally posed. 'Think about it. Are you the optimum person to be making the choices you make, at this time, in this world, to prevent the most number of people from dying and allow the greater number of people to prosper, with no one left behind if at all possible?'

'How could we ever know that?' Gerry spat, forgetting his demeanour. How he hated idealists.

'We can look at the criteria. For example, are you the most unbiased, meek and selfless person available with the mental capacity to perform the role you do?'

'I'm an elected representative! I was chosen by the people!' shouted Gerry, no longer willing to be subjected to this schoolboy lecture.

'This isn't Paxman, Minister' the voice roared back in deep waves. 'Hoist him up!'

A screech of metal against metal filled the room in circular scrapes. Gerry felt himself being pushed up by the chair below him, until only the tips of his toes remained in contact with the ground. As he swayed he heard the chink of iron loops. He wasn't being pushed, his chair was being hoisted up, with him attached. He felt an uneasy sway, his weight shifting and sinking into his seat. It felt like it could break at any moment. Eventually he felt himself stop moving, as something cranked into place above him. Then he felt himself tip forwards. He hooked his feet around the legs of the chair, the binds on his hands and ankles being the only thing keeping him from falling.

'What are you doing?' he shouted down.

'Now, I know it's hard to see in this room, but I can tell you that you are suspended from the floor by your chair, a good twelve feet above the ground. And in case you are disorientated, you are facing the ground. It's not a fall that would kill you. It would probably be your knees that hit first, unless you tilt forwards, in which case it will be your face,' said the raised voice of Uncle, from somewhere below.

'Let me down!' Gerry shouted back.

'Are you sure?'

'No, no no. Okay. What do you want me to say?' Gerry winced as the binds on his wrist started to press into the flesh that wanted to follow the gravity of the situation.

'You see, this is the problem. It's not about what I want you to say, it's about what you actually mean. You've been avoiding straight answers for too long now. So, I will repeat the question. Are you the most meek, unbiased, incorruptible and mentally suited person for the role you are performing in the lives of others?'

There was a hint of impatience in the voice of Uncle rising up from beneath Gerry. This was the endgame. The winch creaked and the chair dipped slightly.

'No! No I'm not.'

'Why not?'

'I don't always act in the best interests of the majority.'

'Whose interests do you work for?' asked Uncle, as if prompting someone through a revision list.

'My own.'

'And?'

'Just my own, I'm selfish...'

The winch creaked again, the chair juddered down another few inches. Gerry gripped tight.

'Okay, okay! And the interest of those who reward me. Sometimes individuals, sometimes groups. People with influence, money.'

'Would you say that I have influence right now?' asked Uncle.

'In this room, yes.'

'That's right. Only in this room. Very good,' Uncle confirmed.

Gerry needed it to be over. One way or the other. He couldn't stand the pain in his wrists and ankles, the fear of the drop, of his face hitting hard concrete at speed, no hands to stop it, or his knees shattering inside his legs.

'What do you want me to do? Give it all up? I will, if you let me live. But why me? I'm just one, I'm not even that senior. If you're after someone on the inside, I'm the wrong man for the job. You're an anarchist, I can see that now. And you're right, the system's corrupt, but it's the best we've got. It works for the most part.'

He had no idea whether to defend his position or yield. Neither had worked to this point, so by now he had disengaged from his attempts to reason or appease. The walls were down.

'How do you know that it's the best we've got when you don't allow people the chance to question it?' Uncle pushed on with his weighted debate.

'But we do! They vote. They have a voice.'

'They vote on the people, not on the system,' ventured Uncle.

'People can rise up. They've done it before, they'll do it again if they have to, if they want to. Killing me won't make a difference. It will just make things worse for you.'

Again Uncle paused.

'What would you have me do instead of this?' Uncle asked, his voice faltering, his texture cracking. Gerry kept on while he had the chance.

'Engage with the system. Use it. That's all we did. It was waiting for us when we were born. It's older than all of us, and it's just a shell, a shell we fill. We're the ghosts in the machine. There is nothing else.'

'Nothing else?' Uncle asked quietly, as if to himself.

'It's just what we make of it. It's what I was brought up to do. It's all I've ever known. And it's empty. It's just us.'

Gerry wasn't sure what his point was, but it was having an effect.

'Like this room?' asked Uncle. 'This room is empty. And it's just us.'

'Yes! And this room has a system, while we're in it. And you're in charge of it.'

'It's a hell of a system,' said Uncle.

Time for the kill, thought Gerry. Whatever he had said, however he had managed it, he was turning this around, fighting warped idealism with warped idealism. It was working, he knew it. Time to turn into the skid, get the vehicle pointing forwards again.

'Are *you* the best person to be in charge?' Gerry asked. 'Are you the least unbiased, incorruptible, fair and merciful person here?'

'You're right. I've made a mistake. This is all wrong,' said Uncle.

Gerry fancied he could hear slow footsteps towards where he believed the door to be.

'Will you let me down then?' he dared to venture again.

'Yes, I think we understand each other now,' replied Uncle. 'I need your help!' he shouted up.

'Whatever you need, just let me down,' Gerry replied quickly.

'Not you. You'll come down. I say, I need your help!' he shouted again.

'Yes, Uncle?' came the voice of the little girl. She was still some way above Gerry by his reckoning.

'Let him down,' Uncle growled.

The girl laughed. The ropes around Gerry's wrists started to shake a little. Like a spider feeling for prey, Gerry could almost discern the toothed metal edge of a knife working them. She must have been closer than he realised. Reaching over from - somewhere. But he was still hoisted!

'Wait no, no!'

The ropes snapped and Gerry sensed the chair moving away from him, or so it seemed. Oddly, as he plummeted towards the ground, the last thing he felt was the relief of finally being off that chair and able to move his hands, though he couldn't move them in time. His face fell inwards and all, once again, was black.

***

In the Upton ward of the Chelsea and Westminster Hospital, a machine beeped not quite every seven seconds. Gerry stirred in his bed.

'How did he do?' said Emma, holding his hand in hers while consulting with her uncle who was busy pressing buttons and taking notes.

'It's hard to tell, until he wakes up. Talking of which, stand back,' Uncle replied.

Emma backed away as Gerry's eyelids twitched ever more rapidly before opening suddenly. His upper body jolted upright while his lower half stayed rigid thanks to the restraints around his waist.

'What? Where am I?' spouted spontaneously from his lips.

'Just relax, Gerry,' said Emma's uncle, 'the interview's over now.' He went back to pressing buttons and ticking boxes.

'Interview?' Gerry's head was still misty, but it was lifting at these words.

'For the next level,' said Uncle, without breaking from his work.

More light shone through.

'You were there! You tied me to a chair! What have you done to me now?' Gerry shifted, unable to move his body, his arms flaying at maximum radius and finding nothing.

'It was just my voice patterns. It wasn't me,' said Uncle, quite unperturbed by the commotion.

'Relax, darling,' said Emma, daring to approach a little closer, though still keeping a very good arm's length away. 'You're back. It's what you wanted, remember?'

'What I wanted? What's what I wanted? Hang on...'

Rather than the fog lifting, Gerry felt like he was driving out of it, leaving it behind. It had always been there, he was just usually above it.

'It's coming back to him. Won't be long now,' said Uncle.

Sunshine. At last.

'This was it, wasn't it? This was the test?' said Gerry, a smile breaking, a beautiful realisation as if waking from a twisted dream to discover the joys of normality.

Emma greeted his smile with her own and embraced him.

'Yes. Thank God. I thought they'd scrambled your brain or something,' she said.

The beauty of remembrance flooded Gerry's synapses. It all came back. 'The next level,' they called it, the latter 21st century's initiation test for the upper reaches of power. The upper echelons, or the 'prime' echelons as he had heard them referred to. He hadn't asked many questions: just to be invited to try was itself a huge honour, a stepping stone. Something to do with possible world simulations - could happen at any time, *you won't know till you are there,* they had told him.

'How did I do? Did I pass?'

Uncle finally turned from his panels and screens. He looked Gerry directly in the eye.

'That depends.'

Uncle was a tall, bald man with glasses. He removed them and placed them on his fleshy gleaming scalp. Gerry had not met him before, though he guessed this was the uncle that Emma had 'had the word with' to get him this far. Funny he should use that term in the simulation, Gerry thought, but still.

'Depends on what?'

'Believe me, Gerry, what you experienced in there was a microcosm of what would happen if we ever really got caught, and if you proceed to the next level, you need to know that. It comes down to a simple choice. Are you in or out?'

Uncle poised his pen above his clipboard and watched Gerry carefully. Before Gerry could answer, Emma squeezed his hand hard.

'What happened, Gerry? Was it painful?' she asked.

'No. Not really. It was just intense.'

'Are you in or out? You must answer now, while the memory is fresh,' Uncle demanded, with the same lack of patience as his simulated counterpart.

Gerry froze, the answer should be simple yet something was stopping him reaching it.

'Gerry this is the next step,' said Emma, releasing her grip and standing back a few paces. 'Real power, remember? It's what you wanted. It's what we wanted. You've worked so hard to get here.'

'In...' said Uncle.

'Or out?' said Emma.

Gerry overrode the anonymous doubt.

'In, I want in. I'll take it.' He breathed out heavily and looked over to Emma. His broad smile soon disappeared.

'Why are you crying?' he asked when he saw the tears break from her eyes. She turned away.

'What? What's wrong? I've said I want it. I want in! I'm ready.'

Gerry laughed awkwardly as he turned to Uncle, hands outstretched, expectant. He waited for the big joke. It didn't come. Uncle moved his pen ever so slightly to the left and made a mark in some secret box.

'Wrong answer I'm afraid, old chap. Sorry, Emma. We'll make sure you and the kids are seen to. We may even be able to make some introductions to future candidates, but not for some time yet; it would seem wrong.'

Emma turned back around and looked straight over Gerry to her uncle.

'Does it have to be this way?' she said.

'He has to truly believe he is doing it for the right reasons. The only answer he should have come away with was no. We can't have people like him at the top. It's too dangerous, and he knows about it now. This is better for everyone.'

'Everyone?' said Emma.

'Well, maybe not everyone. But you're okay, I promised your father I'd see you right, whatever happened. Don't look back,' Uncle said as he pressed a button and the door to the room opened. Without another glance at her husband, Emma left the room.

'Emma? Where are you going? What's he talking about?' Gerry shouted after her, but all he got in reply was the soft hiss of the automatic door closing. He turned back to Uncle.

'I don't understand. What have I done wrong?'

'You know when people wear masks to hide their true identity? Well there wouldn't be much point in a mask that looks exactly like yourself, would there? Sorry, Gerry. Your application for the next level has been denied.'

Uncle pressed yet more buttons and somewhere out of sight a swirl of red mixed with a twist of neon-green. The colours danced together in a glass chamber before gliding away as one through tubes, into their final resting place.

'So let me go then, I won't,' Gerry stifled a yawn that had crept up and made his whole body shudder, 'I won't tell anyone...' His ordeal had been tiring. He yawned again. Little white microbes scurried before his eyes.

'No you won't,' said Uncle as he monitored the steadily decreasing peaks of a line that ran across one of his screens. 'Goodnight Gerry. Sweet dreams. Better luck next time. Well, if you believe in that sort of thing.'

Newsbot Serial One

'It will be a revolution in unbiased news reporting. No longer will we be forced to rely on the unreliable to interpret, filter, prioritise and deliver the vast flow of information that courses through our world every day, every hour, every minute, every nanosecond. No longer will we have to tolerate the interests that distort our vision of this complex and wonderful global civilisation, with all its worries, hopes, triumphs and disasters. There will be no need for blind trust now that we have replaced it with undeniable logic. Responsibility to form opinions and draw conclusions will be returned to the consciousness of the people. News, like science, is observation, evidence, critical analysis and hypothesis. It is science, therefore, that has risen to this challenge and brought you the new herald's of the Earth.

Ladies and gentlemen, I give you the Newsbots.'

The curtain opened, the lights flashed and the crowd roared. In the wings, the inventor cringed at the sight of the screen-faced robots. They looked like hammerhead sharks walking upright on their fins. They had a large rectangular display screen placed upon pneumatic shoulders, and the machines' gait was reminiscent of a rickets sufferer, with knees bent constantly in order to compensate for the disproportionate upper body weight. But worse than the design was the sentiment, the embodiment of his algorithm, as if these machines were actually *the* 'Newsbots', rather than just mechanical hosts for his code. They could just have easily placed a view-screen or phone on a stool. Hell, they could have just 'revealed' a memory stick.

But no, they have to have their moment, even when unveiling the breaker of veils, they had to dress it up a bit. The crowd settled down and the speaker continued.

'Thank you. Now, please welcome to the stage, the inventor of the programme behind the Newsbots, Maverick Jefferson!'

Maverick walked out to great applause and pyrotechnics. They had wanted him to host the whole keynote, for him to don his casual 'I'm normal' clothes and stride up and down the stage, confidently gesticulating as he did so, effortlessly explaining the concept to an ever-frenzying crowd. Having warned them that he wasn't much of a public speaker, he still gave it a go in rehearsals at the sponsor's insistence. It was surprising to see how quickly 'You'll be fine' and 'Don't worry about it' turned into 'Maybe you should relax a little, take the pressure off. We're thinking of bringing in a host so you can just concentrate on explaining the science. How does that sound?'

So here he was, ready to 'do the science'. He stood and waved a little, as practised, moving from stage left to stage right and then back to the centre and behind the small plastic podium with his notes waiting for him. The host, a popular comedian and social commentator by the name of 'Sparky' Bernard, clapped along beside him and alternated the direction of his admiring smile between the audience and Maverick until he judged the moment to be nearly over.

'Maverick, it's hard to believe that there is anyone out there who hasn't already heard about your amazing invention, but maybe you could tell us a little more about how they actually work before we get onto, and I'm so excited about this, the first live demonstration?'

Sparky had reworded the question completely from when they practised little more than an hour beforehand, but Maverick still had his cue.

'Certainly, Sparky, and thank you for such a stirring introduction.'

The crowd erupted into spontaneous applause. Sparky waved his hand in modest dismissal of the praise and gestured back towards Maverick to continue.

'We live in a world of questions, questions we want answering. Sometimes it is hard enough to know what these questions are, let alone find a satisfactory answer for ourselves. We quite literally have information passing through us constantly as the internet is beamed down from satellites and broadcast through our homes and streets by hubs and way stations. Our screens and speakers offer us all the information we could ever need - so much so, in fact, that it is hard to hear for the voices and it is hard to see for all the faces. And we know, at least we believe, that we are not always told the whole truth.'

Behind the stage, above the heads of the dormant robots, a large projection illuminated the auditorium. Scenes of devastation around the world flickered in succession as Maverick continued.

'Were these riots, or protests? Was this terrorism, or a fight for freedom? As the troubles we saw over the last century escalated and spread across the world, the questions also grew. And then, even here in the United States, we faced the question for ourselves.'

The montage ended and was replaced by scenes from the New York uprising. Each black and white clip of the Times Square massacre faded in and out to the sound of a slow heartbeat. No extreme violence was shown. As a baton was raised and came swinging down towards the skull of a protestor, the image faded. As the women and children not strong enough to stand the force of the water-cannons were blasted through High Street windows, the image faded. As the first shots were fired horizontally into the crowd from the black-clad, heavily armoured ranks of private security operatives, the image faded. The scenes continued as Maverick spoke.

'How did it come to this? When did we lose our way? Who is responsible? We turned to our media for answers. We asked them to represent us in the search for truth. But then, what followed just led us further away.'

The image changed again, and now there was an audio feed. A broadcaster, a British broadcaster from the BBC, sitting at her desk, reading the headlines about the American 'riots'.

'Riots continue for a fifth day across several states of America, the most concentrated having taken place in New York's Times Square where reports say a small protest about health-care provision escalated when passers-by witnessed what was described as 'brutality' by private security firms contracted by the Government. Despite a pledge by the White House to bring those responsible for the brutality to justice, riots continued and sparked many sympathy demonstrations in other states.'

The newsreader looks off camera and at her notes. She shrugs.

'Excuse me, is that it?'

She pauses for another second, and places her finger in her ear, listening for instructions.

'That's it? Have you seen the footage? Are we showing the footage? It's a massacre and we give it a hundred words? I know we're live. I don't care.'

She pulls the earpiece away.

'Ladies and gentlemen, not for the first time, I am quite unable to bring you the news and maintain my conscience. If you haven't already, go on the internet, see for yourselves. This is the same security firm recently awarded contracts by our own Government, who, it seems, are not allowing us to tell you about the crimes against humanity being committed...'

She looks nervously from side to side; the film does not show what she can see off camera, but her pace picks up.

'We are bought and sold, we say what we're told. There are more of us ready to tell you. It's time to act! This is not the news!'

The screen goes blank. No one, not even the original audience, ever saw what happened next. By that evening the same news channel was reporting on the mental breakdown of its long-standing presenter and her drinking habits. But it didn't wash, not this time.

The stage projection cut to several fast edited strands of presenters from major networks across the world having similar revelations live on air. Sometimes it was the just the onscreen graphics that were hacked: the slogan, "This is NOT the NEWS", became the calling card of the movement. Pictures contradicting reports were commonly shown, the last defiant acts of behind-the-scenes technicians as they declared support for the movement. The broadcasters that were able to continue relied on extreme audiences sympathetic to whatever cause was funding their operation. In the case of many American networks, the change was hardly noticeable, with aligned newsrooms continuing to openly admit their support by, and for, political parties. For state broadcasters, the transition was brutal and, in some cases, deadly. Many didn't survive the loss of viewers, becoming useless to the state, and closed without mercy or recompense. The ones that did survive changed beyond recognition, as did the governments that endorsed them, opting for open dictatorships and state control over pseudo-democracies and the so-called 'free' press.

In America, the Administration that presided over the massacre of Times Square collapsed. Most senior officials, including the President, were now under arrest, awaiting the trial of the age. In its stead, the hastily assembled 'Free Peoples' party was in control, and had commissioned the realisation of the ground-breaking theories of Maverick Jefferson.

The screen faded out from the last image of the President in handcuffs, ahead of a pack of similarly shackled Senators and Congressmen being led to the old Guantánamo Bay complex in orange overalls. Maverick had kept his head bowed throughout the projection. He didn't turn to watch, having seen it before and not wanting to crane his neck. Also, he felt it a little overblown, as these things always are. A palpable hush remained in the room after the projection had ceased and the spotlight once again rested on Maverick.

'So what is the truth?' he continued, leaving a long pause while surveying the audience from left to right, back to left, and finally to the centre, as rehearsed. 'Is it that we have been lied to before, but the truth is simple? Is it that there are always several interpretations available for any given issue, and we need as much data as possible to decide which is true? Could we perhaps never know the answers to some questions, or even the questions themselves? This is where Newsbots come in.'

Applause.

'When we, the people, took over the structures and frameworks of this country we discovered what we had all feared. Vast apparatus of data gathering and monitoring on a scale that exceeded our worst nightmares. But this revolution was not one of destruction, where we tear down the work of generations just to spite our predecessors, no!'

More applause and whooping. Maverick was getting into his stride, bolstered by the crowd.

'We took that information and we asked just one question: how can this help us? What do we need to understand all this? And so the Newsbots were born. A programme able to analyse all the available data at any given time and respond to any given question with the most likely truth, based solely on analysis of the evidence and tempered by logical representation of alternatives. Installed in units that can present independently or respond to interrogation, both in the community and on our television screens and radios. The next generation of news to help humanity claw its way back from the abyss of misinformation and propaganda and make informed, rational decisions. Newsbot Serial One, please step forward.'

The machine nearest to centre stage behind Maverick clunked forward and positioned itself by the podium. The crowd gasped and cheered. This was the moment: the only true test that could be performed.

'While you have been listening to me speak, watching the films, both here and in the homes of people across America and the world, you have been thinking and talking. We have access to 99% of all conversations in the developed world. Even good, old-fashioned talking is picked up by supposedly dormant devices, constantly connected, constantly feeding back. The methods to harvest this data were not of our design but now it belongs to us again. And so...'

Maverick paused and turned to the Newsbot beside him.

'Newsbot Serial One, query: what at this time is the most common concern of humanity? What question do we want answering?'

'Calculating,' replied the robot in a soft, female, mid-Western American accent.

The Newsbot's screen-face displayed a blue circle that spun to indicate it was processing. For a moment Maverick was concerned that that was all it would do. They had completed this exercise many times, but not with humanity watching and the resulting conversations feeding back and influencing the outcome. The processing needed for such a task, based on Upton-Quantum theory, was extremely advanced and experimental. The spinning light ceased and faded.

'Is Sparky gay?' said the robot.

The crowd roared. Sparky, who had retired to the wings at this point, decided this was a jape of some kind and popped his head out from behind the curtains.

'Hey! That's none of your business, honey!' he shouted across the stage, and gave a wink to the audience who roared again, having barely caught their breath from the last one.

Maverick didn't know what to do. He laughed along. It was just a glitch, an anomaly. Surely.

'Okay! Let's not answer that one, Newsbot. Bit of a joker, I think, ladies and gentlemen. Let's try again. Quiet please.'

The crowd eventually settled down, though occasional titters could still be heard breaking out like radio-frequency interference.

'Newsbot Serial One query.' Maverick thought for a second: he had obviously been too broad before. 'Excluding trivial matters, what is the most common concern of humanity right now?'

'Calcula...' This time the blue circle barely displayed at all. The process completed before the machine even had time to acknowledge. This, however, had the unfortunate effect of causing it to pause for command before answering.

'Then tell us, Newsbot Serial One,' commanded Maverick impatiently. He coiled inside at the thought of another comedy moment. In the wings, some way behind a nervous-looking Sparky, he saw a group of gentlemen, arms folded and staring right back at him. The sponsors.

'Does Maverick Jefferson seek to control and enslave us?' the machine responded alongside a picture of Maverick on the face-screen, surrounded by reams of text and statistics.

'Ahh!' said Maverick, 'a fair question. And one that you can safely answer, for it is questions like these that we were denied answers to before, and I have nothing to hide. Answer, please.'

'Calculating.'

Maverick froze. Why was it taking so long? The crowd began to murmur, the world began to mumble.

'The answer is, most probably, yes,' said Newsbot Serial One, followed by a gasp that sounded like all the air being sucked from the auditorium.

'What? On what basis? Ladies and gentlemen, I assure you this is a fault with the unit. Please observe.' Maverick was thinking fast.

'I have calculated the probability of intentions based on all existing psychological and social records of a Mr Maverick Gilbert Jefferson and cross-referenced the resulting profile against an index of power-to-corruption ratios based on all recorded human deviances from established philosophical and social expectations of just and selfless behaviour following the acquisition or control of major technological advancements,' said the machine.

'Probability? Probability?! You can't judge me on probability!'

'I am designed to reach the most probable truths based on all available evidence. The chance of Mr Maverick Jefferson being corrupted by the specialist knowledge and power he has obtained through the invention of Newsbot processing is high.'

'How high?' spat Maverick.

'99%.'

Another shocked intake from the audience, breaking into jeers.

'But, I, what about the 1%?' By now Maverick was as much pleading to the audience as he was posing another question to the traitorous machine.

'The 1% margin is a built-in threshold based on the uncertainty principle.'

'Of course it is,' said Maverick, remembering his own work and noticing the advancing figures on both sides of the stage.

As he was taken away, to the sounds of the mob, the gentlemen with folded arms looked at each other and realised that they had stumbled upon something that could prove very useful, very useful indeed.

The Beep Next Door

'Beep.'

There it goes again. One, two, three, four, five, six -

'Beep.'

Slightly shorter this time. One, two, three, four, five, six, seven -

'Beep.'

Maybe I'm just counting wrong. It's hard to be accurate. Maybe if I get my phone timer –

'Beep.'

Oh for God's sake! Just ignore it. Bloody beep. What's he got over there? A heart monitor? A fire alarm on a low battery? No, it can't be that. Who would invent a fire alarm that beeps every seven seconds for three weeks when it has a low battery? That's just excessive. Oh hang on, it's –

'Beep.'

... still there. Okay, just blank it out, and get on with your work. Now, where was I? Oh yes.

Daryl struggled against the forces of reality as the machine whirred to life. He was elsewhere. All around him were moments in glass boxes, stretched out as far and wide as the eyes could see. But he had no eyes in this place: he soon realised his vision was absolute, unlimited, dimensionally omnipotent. He could both wander through the glass boxes and inhabit them in the same moment, the only moment, the moment of moments. And they could be changed. They could be -

'Beep.'

Right! That's it. I've had enough. I'm going over there. I don't care anymore. But then, what if it is a heart monitor? Excuse me, Ray, is it? Nice to meet you. Is that a heart monitor I can hear beeping every seven seconds or so through our partition wall? I don't want to be a bother and all, but could you, you know, possibly switch it off and potentially die so that I can get on with my work in peace?

No. That won't do. Just got to carry on, zone it out, like a printer in an open office. Remember those days? You managed to zone out the wittering chatter of a hundred colleagues: surely you can manage a small 'beep' every now and again.

They could be rearranged, they stacked together. Each moment had its entrance and exit points, just like a room. He was now watching a moment, once an old moment, but now happening ad infinitum before him. He saw himself sitting on the grubby brown sofa of a former lover, sharing a cup of tea, smiling and laughing. She smiled and laughed. The edges of the glass box were the doors out of the room. He remembered the feeling, at the time, of not wanting to leave that moment, like the doors would lead him out of something that could never be lived again. But here he was, watching it, as if he could pluck another moment from the air and attach it to the side, coiling his own life and the lives of others into a chain of his choosing. But to <u>not</u> do that, somehow, was the point of it all... The machine beeped.

No! It did *not* beep! Anything but a beep.

The machine whirred...

No, it's already done that...

The machine ticked softly, like a clock you don't realise is in a room until that moment just before sleep when your ear suddenly detects it, and, for a time, you can hear or think of nothing else.

That's better. Time for a fag and a cuppa.

***

In his modest garden, Owen Wagstaff lit another roll-up and took short, sharp, stabbing breaths to get the ember burning evenly. The kettle started its crescendo in the kitchen behind him. The echo of a beep emanated from the ramshackle conservatory next door.

Intrigued to find the source of the penetrating and persistent beep, Owen shuffled from the concrete slabs by his back door over to the soft grass of his lawn. Once he found a good vantage point, he casually drew another breath of bitter smoke and rolled his head as he exhaled, as if working out a crick in his neck. That's when he spotted Ray, the neighbour.

In the two years Owen had lived in Stockwell Place, he had only encountered Ray as a short shock of grey hair atop a fleshy mass that was always hidden behind a fence or bush. But now, through a gap in the blossom, reflecting back from the tinted glass on an open conservatory door, Ray was totally visible as he sat playing with something in his lap.

It was a device of some kind, a TV remote, maybe. Dressed in blue overalls and heavy boots, Ray was red-faced in a struggle with the item he held firmly between his knees while trying to dismantle or loosen it with his hands. As Ray become increasingly agitated with his apparent inability to complete his task, Owen realised the beep had finally stopped.

As he was about to turn away and continue his novel 'beep'-free, he saw Ray collapse and clatter to the floor, bent double over the device he had been struggling with. In an instinctual instant, Owen raced from his garden, down his steep drive, along the street and up the similarly steep drive of his neighbour. He guessed correctly that there would be a side alley by the house that would lead him to the back garden.

He found the conservatory door and went straight in. Ray was not there. There was only the device, a black rectangle, the size of a remote, with just one button. Owen picked it up and examined it. There were no markings, no brand name or compartments for batteries. Just one solitary button, dead centre, rounded and closely fitted. Owen pressed it.

'Beep.'

Owen pressed it again. Nothing. He waited a few seconds. Still nothing. A few seconds more...

'Beep.'

This time he counted for seven seconds before pressing it.

'Beep.'

He did not press it again, and there was no 'beep'. There was no discernible speaker, but the noise had definitely come from the device itself.

There was a clatter inside. The beep once again had distracted him. Where was Ray? Maybe he had crawled in to get help. He had to go in.

The inside of the conservatory was bare, save for a displaced kitchen chair and a forlorn yucca plant wilting in the corner. The door to the house was solid, no window, flimsy metal handle and set into the plain brickwork of the house. He tried it. It was locked.

'Hello! Ray? Are you okay? I heard a noise. Ray?'

He banged on the door and then pressed his ear against the cold wood. He heard scuffles, scraping, and the very slightest 'Shh...'

This was it. What would his hero do? Daryl Upton, the Quantum warrior from his unfinished novel. Upton would go in, knock down the door if necessary. And so, Owen decided, would he.

For once, it was exactly like in the films. The door yielded easily upon his first shoulder barge and swung open to reveal the... the lab?

'Mr Wagstaff, I presume?' said a short, twitching lady in a white coat. She was flanked by two gentlemen, similarly attired, attending to Ray who sat panting at their feet. They were trying to steady him for a breath on an inhaler.

The room was white and sterile, with monitors and equipment running around each edge. There were no dividing walls above or between: it was like a hangar, with the floor space of a semi-detached town house. The only exception was the wall to the left of Owen, which he first presumed was a mirror, but it couldn't be, the reflected furniture being incongruous with the bare floors of the space before him. It looked familiar. Familiarly inverted.

'That's... that's my house,' said Owen, as his cortex finally flipped the image for him.

'Yes it is.'

'Have you been watching me?' said Owen.

'Excuse me,' said the lady before walking over to a panel and holding down a button.

'This is Beta-house 5. We have a problem. The subject is aware, the experiment is compromised. The tester has encountered psychological problems.'

A voice came back through an unseen speaker. The voice was male, deep.

'No. The experiment was a success. Wipe the subject, reset the tester.'

The two gentlemen finally managed to get the struggling Ray to take from the inhaler. He lay down, very still. They approached Owen.

'Mr Wagstaff,' said the lady, 'thank you for your cooperation. The next cycle will start soon. Only three more to go. By then you should have finished the novel as agreed. You'll be made for life. We can promise you that.'

Owen remembered why the words he was writing seemed to flow so easily, save for the distractions. They were his payment, deposited directly in his subconscious for him to eke out over time as if they were his own. All he had to do was inhale deeply and he would forget, again, and in return, the scientists could have their fun.

Scalp

'Do you know how pineapples grow?' said the old man, with the same squinting expression just visible under the semicircular shadow of his protruding flat cap, hands shoved firmly in the pockets of his well-worn green duffel jacket.

'Do they grow underground?' replied Anna, one foot poised on the shovel ready to dig the next sod, just as she had been twenty minutes ago when this impromptu conversation had started.

'No no no,' the old man chuckled, 'that's a common misconception.' His right hand came out of his pocket as if to start pointing at an imaginary blackboard in this seemingly pre-prepared lecture.

'Of course, *part* of them grows underground, you know, the roots, but the fruit, that grows above ground after all the flowering buds on the plant join together.'

The old man seemed happy with himself for having imparted this pearl of tropical botanic wisdom upon his newfound companions. The same couldn't really be said for Colin and Anna, though. They had managed to find a spare hour or two to come up and get some work done on the allotment, and as nice as it was to meet new people, they were running out of time; in Colin's mind, the conversation was beginning to stray into the absurd. It was okay at first: the old man had told them about planting mothballs underneath your cabbages to keep away the slugs and mites, and he had warned them about the local wildlife, especially the pigeons who, he said, line up around the allotments like hungry shoppers going to Tesco's. It had all been very pleasant, but the conversation was one-sided and it was getting strange.

'I shouldn't expect we will be growing any pineapples though, eh? Not in England,' said Colin with a purposeful look around at his plot, and then at his watch.

'Why not? I am,' said the old man. This was the response he had obviously wanted.

'Really? I wouldn't have thought it's possible...' Colin was interested, sceptical maybe, but interested.

'Well not usually. But look, can you see over there? Them polytunnels?'

The old man pointed across to his plot which was more or less opposite Colin and Anna's, separated by a neatly gravelled path. It was early season and, although nothing much was growing, like everyone else's patches, the old man's was well-kept and satisfyingly segregated into even rectangular raised beds. Some beds had neat structures of green netting stretched over old inner tyres that had been cut in half, some had the netting raised a little on tent pegs. Around the edges were the usual sticks inserted into the ground with plastic bottles placed over them to scare the birds away when the wind rattled through. At the far end of his plot, which rose slightly on an incline, was his greenhouse, which from a distance looked like a mini Eden project with big green leaves and bright fruits just visible behind the steamed glass. Below the greenhouse, on the nearside, stood a polytunnel with a semi-transparent plastic covering. There seemed to be life inside that, too, but it was hard to tell. There also seemed to be a network of apparatus set up at both ends, involving plastic tubs and hosepipes that led into the tunnel. There was a kind of a steam rising up in a faint shimmer from each tub. It was the kind of steam that implied a warm, bad smell.

Colin surveyed the plot with the same sense of anxiety he felt whenever he brought his eyes up from his own humble patch of earth and looked around. They were new to the allotment and the winter had eaten half of spring. Their plot had been left wild for a year before they had taken it on in October, so even when the frosts finally stopped, they had a lot of work to do just to find the soil, let alone start planting. They were busy people, both in their early thirties, both with jobs and hobbies besides. Their only aspiration had been to uncover a few metres of earth at least and plant *something, anything,* this season: just to get them started. They hadn't reckoned on the allotment police. The call had come a few days before the encounter with the old man.

'Hello, is that Colin?' asked the distantly familiar voice on the phone.

'Yes, who's this?'

'It's Stephanie, from the allotment'

Ahh, thought Colin.

'I was just wondering if everything's okay?' Stephanie asked, with a good dash of genuine concern in her voice.

'Yeee-s?' replied Colin, stretching the word into a question all of its own. This call had taken him by surprise, as unusual conversations often do. In his mind, the woman from the allotment, whom they had only met twice (once when they first went to look, and again when they picked up the keys), was calling him just to see how he was, which was weird.

'It's just we haven't seen you down here?'

It dawned on Colin that it was going to be one of *those* kinds of conversations that, as you're having it, you simultaneously know that you're going to wish you had reacted differently after it finishes. In Colin's case, that meant he was going to wish he had stuck up for himself a bit more.

'Oh. Well, we have been down there a few times, when we can. We were down the weekend before last.' This was all true, and Colin knew it, but he had offered this as a meek excuse, a feeble concession.

'It doesn't look like you have,' accused Stephanie.

This was the point that Colin would really regret afterwards. His retrospective response would have been 'well we have, you nosy cow,' but instead it came out as a pleading 'we have been down. You probably can't see unless you walk up to it, because we started at the far end away from the path. The end we haven't got to yet is overgrown so it probably looks like we haven't from a distance, but we have, we've planted potatoes.'

'I see. Well, have you paid up with the council? I just wanted to check everything had gone through alright. It's just we've had people before who have never turned up after taking on a plot.' Stephanie was backtracking a little, trying to add a legitimate reason to her intrusive call.

'Yes it's all paid for, and we'll try and get the other end of the allotment cleared if the grass is getting a bit long. Thanks. Bye.'

Colin ended the call, but for the next day or two he would repeat it in his mind over and over. She said, 'we' haven't seen you down there. Who's 'we'? The whole allotment brigade? She accused them of not having worked on it, but if she had bothered to walk over a few metres from the path to the far end, she would have seen that they had. If this is all it takes to warrant a phone call, what's it going to be like for the rest of the year? If they don't get their green netting and raised beds done, if they don't put enough bottles on the ends of sticks, are they going to get a penalty notice through the door? Be marched to allotment HQ for a good going-over? Worst of all, even when Colin and Anna felt like going down there now, they weren't sure if it was because they wanted to, or because they had been told to.

So it was that nearly two weeks later, thanks to the incessant rain, they had finally managed to get to the plot. Despite the phone call from the secretary of the allotment squad, they had convinced themselves it was for their own reasons, but really they were keen to get as much done as possible, even if it was just to make it look like they had done more from all angles. The old man, therefore, wasn't helping.

'You see it? By the greenhouse?' The old man pointed over to the polytunnel flanked by the vats. 'I'm growing them in there.'

'Is that warm enough? I've never heard of a pineapple being grown in England before. At least not in an allotment,' asked Colin.

Now Colin was genuinely interested. One of his plans had been to try out some more unusual growing projects. It didn't look very likely when their main concern was just getting to the soil and they didn't have a greenhouse yet: but one day.

'Not on its own, no. You have to have a heat exchange system, that's what them buckets are for. There's a chemical reaction from the organic matter and the heat is pumped through the tunnel. Just the right amount of humidity and heat is what they need, and that's what I give them.'

'Wow,' said Anna.

She and Colin were not expecting that. The old man had come across as a stoically traditional gardener, British to the core, which was probably made of turnips and spuds. He had already told them that he'd been here forty years, that he used to be the secretary before Stephanie took over, and that he liked to grow wild flowers even though some of the others thought it was a waste of good ground. He had told them about his bad back (made of glass, apparently), his late wife (or so they presumed from his melancholic reflections), his old job as a groundsman at the local cemetery (and how some big strapping lad who started there couldn't hack it after a day), and the mothballs for his cabbages. But now this? A heat exchange system fuelled by a chemical reaction of organic matter? All they had to say for themselves was about the bugging they had got from Stephanie for not keeping up. Given the supposed advanced skills of their fellow gardeners, it almost seemed reasonable now.

'And do you know that if you take the crown off of a pineapple, and plant it, that will give you a whole new plant? If the conditions are right. Fascinating plant, it really is. Well, I better get on, nice talking to you. I'm John, by the way.'

'Yes, I'm Colin and this is Anna.'

They shook hands and John walked away, just as suddenly as he had arrived. He had left on a high, there was no doubt about that. Colin and Anna remained motionless for a moment as they watched him walk to his plot and disappear behind a shed.

'Do you believe him?' whispered Anna.

'I'm not sure that I do, but I'm not sure that I don't either. I'm just glad I've still got some of my ears left.'

'What?'

'Well, he's been chewing them off for the last half an hour.'

Then the rain came and the day was done. They had dug over barely a two-foot by six-foot patch, and not particularly convincingly at that. They waved to old man John as they scurried past back to the car carrying all their tools. The shed on their plot had been sold before they took it over, and anyway, Stephanie had told them that they'd had some problems with kids from the local council estate breaking in, so they were in no hurry to buy a new one. As they drove down the gravelled drive to the padlocked metal gate, they saw John looking intently into his tropical polytunnel while stirring one of the vats with a big gnarly stick.

***

The rain, in typical English fashion, barely stopped for the rest of the week. What was left of spring (after winter had taken a big bite out of it) was turning out to be the usual disappointment. Good intentions or not, there was no point in even trying to get to the allotment, or so Colin had convinced himself. He worked from home mostly, and despite the growing anxiety that had been seeded by Stephanie's call, he wasn't willing to don a mac and try to dig up sludge. The weather would turn, and when it did, so would his attention.

That day came on the Thursday. The rain had dribbled on throughout much of the previous night, and still trickled down in the morning, but the afternoon revealed that rarest of celestial bodies, the sun in all its glory. Colin resolved that if it shone hard and bright for the rest of the afternoon he would venture down to the plots after tea and take advantage of the last few hours of light. Anna would be out anyway, practising with the choir group, so she could drop him off and pick him up on the way back. In his mind Colin would single-handedly transform their humble, jumbled plot into a quadrilateral masterpiece of rich and even earthen beds, free from weeds and grasses, ready to receive nature's bountiful seeds and bring life to life. At the very least, he would sort out the long grass at the path end to keep the plot plods off his back.

The sunlight obliged Colin's plans and beat down relentlessly throughout the afternoon. After a quick and easy dinner of pasta and sauce, Anna dropped Colin at the metal gates with a few select tools and a flask tucked awkwardly under his armpit. It was just after 6 and he had at least two hours of light left to make an impression. With resolve he strode to his plot, making sure to lock the gate behind him. A man on a mission.

The plots were empty - not for the first time. On the half-dozen or so occasions they had been to the allotment there had been very few, if any, other people. Other than old man John, of course. That was what had annoyed him even more about the call from Stephanie. Yes, she hadn't seen them down there, and they hadn't seen her either. *But never mind that*, Colin thought, *I'm here now and by the time I'm finished there will be - kids in the allotment with hoodies?*

Colin spotted them before they spotted him. They were skulking around the patches on the other side of the path: three of them. They all had some kind of hooded attire, though one had his hood down and was wearing a chequered baseball cap. Colin retreated behind the nearest greenhouse and peeped out to see what they were up to. The thought crossed his mind that they might be perfectly legitimate gardeners, and that his preconceptions could possibly be unfounded and shallow. Then one of them lit a cigarette and took the flame from the lighter to the leaf of a rhubarb plant. Unless this was some unusual practice to encourage pollination, he figured they weren't there to dig potatoes. What should he do? He could go over and challenge them, but they looked, even from a distance, to be as tall as him, if not taller, and doubtless fuelled with the angst of youth that he had long packed away along with his drinking. He didn't have his phone, and even if he did, would the police come? Can you be arrested for grievous vegetable harm? For now he resolved just to keep an eye on them from his hiding spot behind the greenhouse - filled with surprisingly ripe tomatoes for this time of year. If they looked like they were going for a shed, then he would do something. That would be the limit.

For a few minutes they stood around smoking the same fag, or was it? Whatever it was, they were sharing it. Probably weed, Colin reckoned. At least they might just get stoned and move on. A bottle came out from somewhere and they all chugged at the pissy-looking contents. Cheap cider, most likely. Not a good sign. Potheads he could deal with, popheads he couldn't. After they had drained the bottle dry they dispatched it with a drop kick into someone's radishes. They didn't even have the courtesy to plonk it on the end of a stick. Then they started to move. They had spotted something: John's vats, by the pineapples.

Oh shit, thought Colin. During the sodden week he had looked at pineapple-growing in the UK on the internet. All he had really found was one estate that had reared a pineapple that was estimated to be worth £10,000 because of the amount of care and resources it had taken to grow in this climate. He had hardly believed it at the time, and he still wasn't sure if there really were pineapples in John's tunnel, but if there was, the last thing they needed was three teenagers kicking them in. Or three teenagers kicking *him* in for that matter, but if there was any truth to the old man's tales, they could be about to cause more damage than they could possibly imagine. He had to do something, and quick: they were already messing about with the stick in one of the vats, flicking the thick gunk that clung onto it and trying to dunk each other in.

Colin imagined how it would go down. He would shout out and stay hidden. If they didn't move he would take his shovel in hand and approach slowly, shouting all the way. They would, of course, bolt like startled stallions and make for the nearest fence, which was behind them. This plan formed in an instant except for one detail: what should he shout? Should he make a guttural roar and try to baffle them away? Or swear and scream? Should he threaten? He settled with, 'Oi! You! What you up to?'

He ducked back down behind the greenhouse and peeked out slowly, presuming they were looking his way. They hadn't moved. They were just standing there, all looking down at the polytunnel. Colin grabbed his shovel in one hand, and in some subconscious throwback to the many action movies he had watched, tucked a trowel into his pocket as back-up. He walked confidently and erect around the greenhouse and made a beeline towards them, shouting as he went.

'What are you doing here? Get out of here. I'll call the police. Go on, get out!'

Still they stood there, just looking down into the tunnel. As Colin approached he could see that one of them had either cut a hole or lifted a flap. The top was open and John's pineapples were probably dying with every second of exposure to the mild northern air. He broke into a run and before he realised how fast he could move under stress, he was upon them. There was no way they couldn't hear him now but still they just stood there. Even when he was right behind them, all huddled around the hole in the tunnel, they didn't turn to him. Colin soon found out why.

Colin looked over the shoulders of the boys who, now that they were closer, were actually a lot smaller than his fear had portrayed them. Inside the tunnel he saw the *plants*. Were they plants? The 'leaves' emanated outwards from a slightly convex and pale central circle and were light, thin strands, bunched together in tufts. He could see three plants through the gap and they were all different colours and textures. The one directly below him was curly, black and thick. The one on the left had smooth and golden leaves, undulating slightly like a gentle wave. On the right-hand side they were auburn and seemed to be platted together at the stem and frayed and tangled at the edges. He had seen this before somewhere but not here, not like this, and it bothered him, but not as much as the growth at the centre of each plant. Smaller stems, more tubular than the leaves, and pulsating slightly, had converged in the middle, and the end of each had intertwined to form a central sack or pouch. It was translucent and covered in thin blue lines that stretched all over the membrane. It, too, was pulsating from within. Moving. Little bumps appeared here and there around the edges, stretching the pink covering and causing it to go white for a moment before retreating back and trying again somewhere else.

'What are they?' asked one of the lads who had unflinchingly accepted Colin's presence at his side and didn't break his stare.

'I don't know,' Colin replied.

'It looks like hair,' said another of the boys.

Yes, that's it. That's where he had seen it before. Colin had a brief moment of relief, as when one finally identifies the word dangling from the tip of the tongue, but this was soon replaced with a new moment of puzzlement. It *was* hair, and suddenly, with this piece in place, the rest of the construct started to make sense. The rounded circle that it grew from, that was a scalp, a goddamn scalp, in the ground. The tubes that ran up from it were veins, pulsating, it can only be presumed, with blood. The only thing that wasn't immediately identifiable was the fruit in the middle. Colin cast his mind back to the numerous documentaries he had seen of mammals falling out of grunting mothers, still covered in the membrane of a birthing sac. It couldn't be, it was impossible. It was moving.

'I think something's trying to get out,' said the boy to his right, daring to lift a shaky finger in the direction of the thing below.

One of the white bumps stretched out again, much further than before: it came to a small point that looked ready to split like rubber stretched over a pin. The boys and Colin stood mesmerised, awaiting the arrival of, of whatever it was...

'Get off my land!'

The voice burbled out from a shape that rose up out of the vat beside them. It was covered in a thick brown and black goo that cascaded down what was quickly becoming its head, and glooped and gathered in folds on its shoulders. It lifted a dripping arm that stretched out and seized the nearest boy.

'Get it off me! Get it off me!' he cried, unable to get a purchase on the slimy appendage.

The other boys rushed to his help but also found themselves caught. It seemed the ooze was drying rapidly anywhere it came into contact with them, and they couldn't break free. Colin circled with his shovel in hand, trying to figure out the best place to strike without hitting the captives. Keeping as far away as possible and getting behind the creature, he lifted his shovel high in the air and made ready to bring it down on its head.

'Stop!' came a voice from behind him. It was the old man John, limping down as fast as he could with hand outstretched.

Still holding his shovel aloft, as if set in time, Colin turned to see John approaching. He had slowed down to a gentle stroll now and put his hands back in his pockets. He looked calm, but then, why shouldn't he be, realised Colin: these were his monsters, after all. Colin turned around to finish the job but the struggle was over. The form had sunk back down into its viscous hole and the boys collapsed on the ground, unmoving. John walked straight past Colin and looked at the boys.

'Bloody kids,' he said, before taking the nearest to him by the ankles and dragging him across to the vat at the opposite end of the tunnel. 'Still, good feed, though. Give us a hand.'

'A hand doing what?' asked Colin. He let his shovel fall to his side, too baffled to make any assumptions.

'Getting him in here. While he's fresh,' said John, nodding to the vat.

'But you'll kill him!' Colin reached again for his shovel.

'Bit late for that, I'm afraid,' said the old man while lifting up the wrist of the boy at his feet for a moment before letting the arm drop loosely and lifelessly to the ground.

'Oh my God! What have you done?' Colin gripped the shovel in both hands but remained where he was, considering the old man with newfound fear and wonder.

'Well, if you'd only give me a hand we might still have time for all of them. Put that shovel down, actually, don't bother. Dig me three holes just here, in line with the tunnel, while I do this.'

'You want me to dig their graves?' Colin spluttered.

'Graves? No no no. Just a few inches down should do it - about, hmm, this wide.'

The old man held up his hands and formed a broken circle with his fingers and thumbs, after roughly comparing it to the size of the boy's head. Then he took out a flick knife and gently turned the head of the boy at his feet so that the ear was facing him. He kneeled down, held the head steady in one hand and moved in gently with the knife in the other.

'Stop it! Stop it!' yelled Colin. He leapt across with his shovel and brought it across hard onto the old man's side. He didn't have it in him to bring it down on his head.

The old man put an arm up in defence which took the brunt of the impact, but he was still knocked sideways to the ground, sending the knife one way, and the hat on his head the other. That's when Colin saw it, his scalp, or rather, his lack of scalp. Just above the ears a line of scar tissue ran around the circumference of his head, and above that the thinnest of skin coverings was left. It had the same translucent quality of the sacs in the plants, but it wasn't undulating. Beneath it, Colin could only guess, was the skull, but the hair and scalp had gone.

'Now what did you go and do that for?' asked the old man, picking himself up and scrabbling around for his hat and knife. 'Do you want these boys to live again or not? We haven't got much time. Get digging.'

Perhaps it was the sheer weight of extraordinary events, but something inside Colin's head just lay down and gently gave up the fight. He had no sense of right and wrong in this situation, no reference material, no comparisons to draw on. His inner voice was useless, and the only other voice was that of the old, scalped man, who seemed to know what he was doing. This was his world.

Colin dug the holes while the man carefully removed the scalps of the boys. Together they placed the bodies into the vat that had not hosted the strange creature. All Colin remembered was how he didn't think they would all fit in, but as each one was lowered down, they seemed to dissipate and join the thick mulch. In each of the three holes the old man placed one of the scalps so that the crown just crept over the surface and the hair was exposed. He nipped into his greenhouse and returned with a length of hosepipe. He placed one end in the vat where they had disposed of the bodies and wove the length of the pipe around the newly planted scalps. He sucked at the free end until the ooze flowed through, and then placed this in the vat with the monster. With his flick knife he poked holes in the pipe around where they had placed the scalps and the ooze gently trickled onto the ground around them and soaked down. So far so good, thought Colin as he watched the old man scurry about with bits of plastic and canvas to build an annex off from the main tunnel and over what was now left of the boys. Colin calmly held the parts in place while the old man stretched and clipped the canvas together with cable ties and hammered pegs into each corner. When they had finished, Colin had an unusual sensation of a job well done, which made him feel slightly sick.

'That ought to do it. With any luck, they'll root down. I'll get a better shelter up tomorrow, but this'll do for now.'

Colin and the old man were both sitting on the floor beside the new addition to the tunnel. The sun was just dipping down and casting long, thin shadows around them as if they were the centre of their own living time dials.

'What happens now?' asked Colin, for several reasons.

'Well, if they root, they'll grow. If they grow, they'll flower. And if they flower, they'll fruit! I'll have to get some more vats, mind. Only room for one at a time once they've fruited. It helps them grow, it swells them up. I can go from fruit to fella in a season, all being well.'

'But what will they be like?'

'Like? They'll be like they were, only better. I think. Yes, usually better. It's all down to the feed.'

'How do you know?'

It suddenly dawned on Colin that all he may have taken part in over the last hour was the disposal and scalping of three boys with a maniac who thinks nothing of taking a knife to himself. Then he remembered the form in the ooze.

'Is that... in there...?' Colin asked as he craned around to look at the vat which bubbled as if in response.

'Me? Yes. I'm nearly done. In there and out here. This old body of mine, it's done okay, but it was a bad season when I was grown. Lots of rain. The bones never properly hardened up. Forever to the doctor's, I am. Got me own seat there! And I can't shift this infection I've had on me chest. You know, the same as me wife had.'

'What happened to her? Didn't you, you know...' Colin nodded towards the polytunnel.

'I don't know. Was years back, before my time. I think it was me great-great-grandfather was the first. It may even have been what happened to the wife that led me to find all this out.'

'You mean, you're not the first?'

'Oh no! Fifth generation, me. Just like the pineapples, we keep on growing back, only difference is we can plant ourselves. Much easier.'

'Do you remember?'

Colin's fascination was no longer morbid or born from shock, it was extraordinary and grounded in the advancement of humanity.

'Bits and bobs. But I was lucky, I got to meet the last one for a little while before he passed on. He told me all he could remember. Sometimes we don't have long and only bits get passed down. But there's all the stuff at the house, in the attic mostly, so if I ever want to fill in the gaps, I can go exploring.'

'But this is, this is unbelievable! You're saying that you've propagated yourself for generations. Perfect clones? This could change life as we know it. There's so much I want to ask. How did you find this out? How does it work?'

'I can only answer one of those, I'm afraid. However we found this out, well, that's lost with the pages it was written on. There was a book, I know that much. All that's left now is the cover. "Top secret – keep out", that's all it says. How it works, well, that's all down to the feed. It's a chemical reaction of organic matter. The more organic matter the better, really. All that energy, it's what they need. Especially now there's three more to grow. You need at least twice the amount to each plant. It's a shame, really.'

Colin fiddled with a dandelion that he had plucked out from the earth beside him. He had images of a new world, a world where you could grow your own you. A kind of immortality, he thought. And he had discovered it here, in the allotments. But there was a niggle fighting its way through from the back of his mind that had been subdued until now by the events of the day. It grew into a fully formulated warning; like the monster from the vat, it emerged slowly and surely out of the thick tar of his consciousness. He stood up, not too quickly, and casually picked up the shovel as if to sling it over his shoulder and go home for the night. No sudden movements, he thought.

'The other three,' Colin asked tentatively, trying to disguise the trepidation in his voice, 'the ones that are already growing. How did they come to be here? Who are they?'

'Them? Well, you know one of them. At least I guess you've met Stephanie?'

The auburn haired plaits: he remembered now where he had seen them before.

'She took over as secretary of this place. Forced me out, really. I was off my feet for a few weeks and she moved in. All I could do to keep this plot was let go of control of the whole place. She's a little go-getter, that one. But she'll be better, when she's grown. I talk to my plants, it helps them grow, and it sticks with them, you know. Aye, she won't be bothering you again.'

By now Colin was pretty sure of the main ingredient of the magic feed, and it didn't sound like the old man needed to wait for a happy accident to get it. Colin edged a few spaces back, enough to swing the shovel if needed.

'And the others?' he ventured.

'Not everyone puts in their fair share around here. I know Steph got on your back, but you've only just started! And with them frosts and all. No, you need more time. But some of them, well, they just keep letting things grow out and spread out and seed, and ruin the place. It's more than just your own plot, you know? It's a shared space. We can't be having people let the place down. The last couple, who had your plot, they were like that. But they won't be, and I'm sure when they come back there'll be another plot free for them. If they want it.'

The old man picked himself up from the ground and seemed to notice for the first time that Colin was now standing with his shovel raised and his eyes wide, watching his every move.

'How do you explain it? Aren't they gone for months?' asked Colin, thirsty now to learn all he could before the inevitable.

'Oh, we're careful to make sure we only pick the ones who won't be missed by too many folk when we can. These boys will be a problem, but between us, we'll figure it out.'

The old man was smiling and advancing one small step at a time towards Colin.

'When there's enough of you to corroborate the occasional sighting, missing people aren't really that missing, just absent. And then they come back, happier than ever, and very, very productive gardeners. Just look around.'

And that's when Colin saw it. He'd seen it before, but now it made sense and it put his earlier anxiety in context. The plots all perfect, all maintained to such a standard. Even so early in the season the plants that were growing were strong and healthy: each greenhouse hinted at shades of green, red and yellow, bustling with ripe tomatoes, peppers and chillies. The beds were even and weed-free, all perfectly edged up to the network of neat grassy paths that ran throughout the pleasingly proportioned strips of deep earth. It was a divine allotment, as if tended by Heaven's gardeners. In this light, it looked like a vision of Eden in the early throes of spring, getting ready to burst to life and assault every sense with its pungent veracity.

'You're not going to let me go, are you?' said Colin. The time had come, and he set his right foot back a pace or two to steady himself for a swing of the shovel.

'Who? Me? Or me?'

Old John pointed behind Colin. His undeveloped self was rising from the sludge once more, again to the cry of 'Get off my land!' Colin quickly decided to go for old John first, but, as he swung back, the monster caught the end of his shovel from behind. Colin turned quickly, waltzing below the shovel and spinning to face the monster. He struggled hard to pull the shovel free but the slime was hardening down the handle and getting ever closer to his hands. He quickly reached into his pocket and grabbed the trowel he had stowed back when all his problems amounted to was a small group of stoned teenagers. He threw it at the black form and it struck the side of the head, causing it to loosen its grip long enough for him to wrestle control back over the shovel which he immediately swung around to fend off old John who was nearly upon him with his flick knife in hand. Old John stumbled backwards over the new polytunnel, fell, and remained quite still. A tributary of blood ran from somewhere below his skinless head, through the uneven earth towards the growing scalps. Behind Colin the vat bubbled and erupted.

***

Anna arrived at the gates at around 8.30pm. It was later than she had expected, thanks to the overzealous choir leader's insistence that 'just one more time round and we'll nail it! Come on!' But she was here now and was surprised not to see Colin. She waited a few minutes while the song on the radio finished playing before getting out to have a look. She didn't have a key, and it was getting dark. She was not best pleased, but then, maybe Colin had just lost track of time. She reached for her phone and was a button press away from calling him when a shadowy figure came jogging down the path towards her from the other side of the gate. The light now hung so low in the sky that it didn't make it up as far as the high-fenced lane to the allotment.

'Colin? Is that you? Hello?' she called out.

'No no no. He's gone.'

It was the old man, John, Anna remembered. He seemed out of breath.

'Are you okay?' Anna asked. They stood facing each other through the square gaps in the metal fence.

'I thought I saw your headlights. He asked me to let you know that he wasn't feeling very well and he's headed home.'

Old man John panted and put his hands to his knees.

'With all his tools? Are you sure you're okay?'

He waved his hand in protest at her concern.

'I'm fine, just catching my breath. I've got your tools in my shed. You might even catch him if you set off now. Go on. He looked a little peaky to be honest. Go on now.'

Old man John took off his cap, turned and receded, into the shadows. Anna got back in her car and headed home. As she drove she wondered whatever was the matter with Colin. She also wondered how she had never noticed the old man's thick, bushy hair before.

The Day the Stars Moved

Coleen opened the door as softly as she could manage, teasing out the lock mechanism and placing her finger over the catch to release it gently as it flicked out of the wooden cradle. She stepped through the smallest gap she could manage and closed the door behind her. She was out.

The routine with the door was overcautious perhaps, but how it clattered if you just went blundering through. The glass shakes and rattles in the frame, the handle squeaks ferociously, and the lock clunks and clicks at a surprising rate of decibels. Coleen didn't want to wake her parents. Not out of courtesy, mind, out of caution. She was going for a smoke.

Nineteen years old and still sneaking around for a cigarette. She didn't want to end up like her cousin Michelle. She's nearly thirty and Auntie Em still doesn't know she smokes. No, that's not what she wants. She will either give up before they find out, or come clean, one day. But not yet, not while she's still living under their roof, eating their food.

Luckily for Coleen, her parents were early and heavy sleepers. Dad was usually shattered from a long shift at the cheese factory, and her mum usually kept the same hours. Even though she didn't 'work', she would busy herself between 7am and 3pm, then start getting dinner ready. Dad always came in starving, and though he wouldn't mind if tea wasn't on the table, he loved the fact that it was. Fair play, though, he has been packing cheese for nearly ten hours. ('Cheese, cheese everywhere, and not a bite to eat,' he would often say.)

Coleen stepped out and around the corner of the house. The window to her parent's room was always slightly open, so if she lit up by the back door the smoke would weave like a wispy snake up into the room directly above. It had all the world to go at, but it always chose to go exploring the window, teasing at discovery. So now she stood around the corner, kept out of sight from the street by her dad's car in the driveway and safe from the window (though she still fancied some of the smoke would make sharp turns to go and seek it out, so she exhaled extra hard in the opposite direction to be absolutely sure).

It was dark, and not too cold. Summer was hanging on for all its worth, but it couldn't hold back the nights which crept up to quash thoughts of endless seasons. Coleen liked the dark nights even if it did mean Summer was on the wane. The early true black of Autumn and Winter felt *proper*, like you could easily tell when evening began and the day stopped. Nights out were better in the dark. It was like having two days in one, rather than one long day that fades out eventually. You take off your day clothes, you put on your nightclothes, you go out, you stay in, whatever. The point is that your brain knows the difference when the sun dips suddenly and early. One is over, the next has begun. Much better, if not so warm.

She lit her Marlboro Red with a match. Matches are easier to explain than lighters. The first puff brought her a lungful of phosphorus mixed in with the tobacco. She stifled a cough, holding her hand to her mouth and containing it within the back of her throat. Little streams of smoke came out of her nose. She smiled.

The cigarette burned away quickly in her hand between breaths. Smoke is blue. That can't be right. Someone had told her that years ago, but she hadn't believed them. But it is, in the right light, or lack of it. Blue like fabric softener. She watched the blue spiral in thick slugs towards the sky, and she saw the stars.

She craned her head back and took them in. It was a clear night. Another reason why dark nights are better: you see more stars. If you get a really dark, clear night, you see hundreds. And the longer you look, the more you see. And if you look for long enough and relax your eyes, they're like those old magic eye pictures that her parents still have hanging around on the bookshelves (apparently they were popular in the 1990s). They don't form anything, but they shift, and you see the depth.

All of a sudden, this little pinprick of light, billions of light years away, possibly not even there anymore in time, has depth against the others. Is it really possible that the eye can tell which ones are closer, all this way away? It makes you dizzy if you do it too long, it makes your head spin. Though that may just be the blood gathering in the back of your brain from having your head tilted backwards so long. Coleen imagined her head like a water balloon filled with red liquid and laughed quietly.

Her cigarette was over so she carefully fed it through a slot in the gutter drain. A gutter for an ashtray, she thought: hardly makes her feel like an adult, which allegedly she is now. No. First year out of college and she still felt like a child, only now she had nothing to do. Yes, she was applying for jobs, but just how many jobs exactly can one apply for with nothing else to do at all, all week, every week? She knew her way around the computer, she had her CV ready to go before she left college. The first two weeks after leaving she had identified nearly every office junior role in a twenty-five-mile radius and sent off applications. Checking the boards now only took five minutes. Email alerts told her when a new posting was up: a quick glance confirmed if it was something worth applying for, and if not, that was her day done.

Adulthood was boring so far, but she figured that's because she wasn't really an adult. She had no bills to pay, no job to go to, and consequently nowhere to live (aside from with her parents, but that doesn't count, they're obliged up to a point, and anyway, who else would she live with?). Is this it? Is this all she has to look forward to in this life of hers? She hadn't bothered with university. The subjects she had chosen at A-Level were boring enough even for two years, taking one of them to the next level for another three, well, that just seemed like a prison sentence. Yes, there would be parties and drinking and friends in some city or other, but then there would also be debt, anxiety, business studies. For three years. No, that wasn't happening.

Instead she had chosen the 'stay at home and work' option. A few of her friends had done the same, and they went out now and again, even if it was to the same places they'd been going to, for the last few years anyway (Valentino nightclub, drink all you can for £10, Thursday night student special – free entry for 'ladies'). But surely they would soon break out of that, as they got older and wiser, and more discerning with their social choices? To be honest, it wasn't looking likely. The pattern was set in. Round to Shelly's house for a bottle of vodka and cranberry between them while her parents were still out, fall into a taxi, arrive in town half-cut, get in the club early, warm spirits from plastic glasses, sticky carpets, get off with someone (usually that Mike from the year above them in sixth form), argue over the taxi fare home after blowing it on kebabs and chips, stop on the way at an ATM, get back to Shelly's, sleep in her bed (top to tail) and repeat, every week.

It was a wonder she hadn't started on the drugs yet from sheer boredom. She had the chance. The other girls who dodged uni, Steff and Rach, had been doing pills for a while. It was funny at first, watching them dance and gurn, gurn and dance, telling her they loved her, that she was like, 'all cosy and safe and beautiful, just like these pills', but it soon wore off. The fake sentiment, the dodgy blokes honing in on the pillhead girls. Losing track of them as they went off somewhere, back to a party with some strangers. No. It wasn't for her. Nowadays they just didn't go to the same clubs. Rach and Steff went to 'Breaks', a dingier, louder place, full of hugging chemheads.

Boys weren't really of interest. She had yet to meet one in a setting and situation that led to anything other than a fumble in a dark place. Maybe Mike was nice, but outside of vodka-induced horniness, she never met him in the 'real world', nor did he ever ask her, which she reckoned said a lot about him. No, she wasn't bothered for now, not like this, not in this near catatonic state of boredom and repetition.

She lit another fag. Her plan had been to stand out here for a while until the smoke smell faded from her baggy T-shirt, but by now, she realised, she wanted another. Funny thing, addiction, just keeps on coming back.

She craned her head to the stars once again. She fancied she saw one move. She tracked the trajectory, one straight line, slightly curved - a satellite, no wonder. Funny, that, she thought. If I were an alien, visiting Earth, I would make sure my craft looked like a satellite. I bet before, when people saw them zigzagging all over the place, they hadn't figured it out, or we didn't have enough satellites in the sky. Now, if they were here, they would definitely try and look like a satellite, 'cos you see them all the time. Or the space station. We'd never know.

What am I going to do with my life? was the next thought to fill her mind. How am I ever gonna break out of this? Named after some stupid celebrity from before I was born. I love my parents, but they're hardly mould-breakers, except literally in Dad's case. A cheese-packer and a housewife. Wow. What a start in this 'don't-let-anyone-know-you're-clever' neighbourhood. Friends who don't seem to want anything to change, either. The conversation never comes up. As long as they can get pissed/stoned/shagged every week or so, they seem happy enough. Working in an office for some company I don't give a shit about? In a job I just *know* will be boring? Just so I can get my own place a few miles, or metres, down the road? Goddamn it.

The darkness was swelling inside her as it often did. She felt talented, though she wasn't yet sure why. She had dabbled and was pretty good at art, but nothing compelled her. She liked music, but who doesn't? She had never learned to play anything. Anyway, all her mates are into chart music. You don't exactly 'learn' how to play chart music, some geeks stitch it all together somewhere and just bring in a bimbo to front it. She'd been asked once, by Jim from her Media Studies class: he liked to call himself 'DJ Undercut'.

'Can you sing?' he asked her, having just burst into the common room and stomped straight over to where she was sitting playing 'Guess Who?' with Shell.

'Dunno. A bit,' she had answered, modestly. She actually had a very nice voice.

'You wanna sing on my new track? Doing a club mix – want some vocals, you know just samples. And a video, we're doing a video, too. Got the camera from Miss Thompson, for my project.'

Turned out that DJ Undercut's idea of a video (which he wanted to shoot before she had been anywhere near a microphone) was going to involve a car (his 'classic' Nova), a bucket (his mum's bucket), some soapy water (from the good people of Persil) and a fair amount of car washing with unorthodox parts of her body. She said 'No' almost as soon as he held up the sponge and asked her why she wasn't wearing her bikini.

No, singing wasn't it, or at least she had no idea how to go about it and what she would do.

'I feel as dark as the sky,' she muttered aloud, the words mingling with a cloud of smoke.

She was still looking up. She recognised some of the constellations. The big dipper, Orion's belt... Well, that was about it. She knew that Orion's belt was presumably a smaller part of something bigger, being a belt and all, but couldn't pick it out. Maybe she could see some shoulders up there, but maybe not. Definitely not. The star she was looking at was moving. Another satellite. And another was moving on the other side. No, that must be a plane, it's way too fast, isn't it?

Then, as she stared and squinted, the whole sky, every dot and sparkle, started to move all at once. Some spiralled, some zipped to and fro, some dipped like yo-yos. The whole universe was dancing around. Colleen looked away, testing her vision against her hands, against the brickwork of the wall behind her, the cracks in the tiles below. Nothing was wrong with her eyes, everything else wasn't moving. She looked up again.

The stars still moved. There were so many to see. If she didn't focus on any particular one, they looked like germs under a microscope, trundling randomly about a Petri dish. But if she did look, they were all doing different things. Some clumped together and flocked like distant birds in various stretched circles, others just kind of swung like a pendulum or seemed to shake really fast.

How could this be? These weren't actually dots. These were gas giants in other solar systems. What she saw as movement here would be devastating, immense forces at the source. This sky, like this, it wasn't real, it couldn't be real, yet here she was seeing it. If she was seeing it, so must everyone else. Should she run up to her parents, wake them, show them? Should she try and film it. Her phone was inside and...

It stopped. She had looked away for the briefest moment to deposit her cigarette into the drain, having burned down to the filter and tickled her fingers with falling ash. When she looked back, same old sky. Once inside the house, a quick check of the TV and internet confirmed that if anyone else had seen it, they hadn't told anyone.

No. It just couldn't have happened, thought Coleen. The stars don't move and dance, and if they did, even only for a few seconds, why me? She went to bed after washing the yellow stains from her fingers and switching off the living room lights. She checked once more through her bedroom curtain. The stars remained still and never moved again, not for Coleen or anyone else. She was the only witness, she never mentioned it again. She lived a long and average life, but she was happy, in the end.

The Voice of Strad

Dearest Paolo,

Do not tell the others, but I must express my joy and, I should say, relief at news of your engagement. Finally! A Stradivari boy takes the plunge! I thought it was never going to happen. I often think it is my fault that Francesco or Omobono never settled down in such a way. I must admit, there are many ways to honour your father, and yes, following his trade is one and I don't begrudge your half-brothers that, but another, as you have now proved, is making one's own path. (How is the cloth business? Still keeping you well?) And I love you all for it, but at least your path will keep our name alive in flesh and blood (I presume that little feet will soon follow?).

Yes, it has weighed on my mind rather a lot recently: continuation, legacy. I am an old man now, Paolo, and it seems my instruments are aging with me. I don't mean the ones I have already made, of course they age, like wine: no, I mean my new creations. They are not the same, you know. I'm sure you've heard it said, and I think it is true, though I would ask you not to repeat this, for the business, the families' sake you understand.

Yet, I feel no less able in mind and body than ever before, but it is the little things, like my very own wrinkles and drained hair, that seem to keep sneaking through into the weft, the tone and balance. Little imbalances, like my own, keep emerging. It is like the wood has warts that cannot be smoothed by the sharpest plane, even though it appears so on inspection. There is a little of me in everything I make, I come to realise now, and that has weighed on my mind, especially after a rather strange encounter.

At your mother's behest I was taking a little air. She thinks the loft is devoid of it, I'm sure, but I know better than to argue. I am that wise at least! So I found myself taking a gentle stroll down to the Torrazzo, taking in the sights and sounds of Cremona in the bitter throes of winter. It is beautiful still, do you remember? It is as if Leonardo himself paints it each season anew, with nature's palette. I stopped for some refreshment, I don't mind telling you, a drop or two of grappa to kill the coffee no less. If your mother will make me take these little adventures on my own, then it is only fair I choose the manner of my indulgences. Anyway, it helps with the cold, or at least it numbs the body!

As I nursed my second 'corrected' espresso in the *cafe Alto Villaggio* I was joined by a most unusual man who went by the name (excuse the rendering, it is not a name I have heard before) – *Froggattio*. He was inquiring as to his whereabouts, which I found rather a strange conversation.

"Can you tell me where I am?" he asked, slowly, though in perfect Italian, despite his clunky English accent.

"You are here," I replied, not meaning to be sarcastic, but all the same, "Where else could you be?" I asked, genuinely confused by his question, you understand.

"But," he continued, "where is *here*?" At this point, I would have thought perhaps too much grappa had rendered this strange Englishman temporarily insane, if it were not for his demeanour, which was sober, if agitated.

"This is the Piazza del Comune," I assured him, "have you got lost? Do you need directions?"

The man seemed no more appeased with knowing his own location once he had learned it. He bashfully inquired further.

"Could you perhaps tell me *when* this is? In time?"

I point out the location of the clock tower, not having my timepiece with me, and ventured that it was around mid-afternoon, if that helped. But hear this, Paolo, if you will believe me, he wanted to know what *year* it was! Days, yes, I can accept people lose track of them. Maybe even the month, if it so happens that the day you have lost track of falls betwixt two, but the *year*? And this was no senile, doddering man like myself; no, this was a man of middle age. If he was mad, then his madness didn't stretch to his attire or hygiene. His skin was quite unlike any Englishman's I had seen. His teeth shone.

I decided to humour the man, and I told him this is the year 1736, for this was early last December.

"I've gone forward!" he said. "Maybe I'll keep going forward and get home!"

I agreed, and commented that that was usually the way of things. He seemed all of a sudden relieved. He laughed and asked my name. I told him. I soon noted the wrinkle of recognition in the lines of his forehead as he reached for the connection. "The violins," I added, to help him along.

Now, I know this all seems no more than a chance encounter with a confused man, and, despite its fair strangeness, is not that extraordinary, but it is what he said next that was most intriguing.

"I know you!" he said, sitting down rather presumptuously opposite. "Yes, you make the most beautiful violins, don't you? At last! Something I remember."

This was not so strange, until: "Oh, your instruments, they are the best in the world, in all of history I shouldn't imagine. I once watched a programme on the glowing picture tube box about your violins. Is it the Messiah or something? One of your best? Worth millions, I heard."

I didn't quite follow his ramble. I knew not what a glowing picture tube box was, nor how he could watch, rather than read, a programme. I pointed this out. He said, "glowing picture tube" to me again and asked me to repeat it. I did. He said something about it being strange how that happens when he says words not yet invented. Something is translating for him, he said, and he's not sure how it works, but it gets mixed up with certain nouns.

Regardless of this linguistic quirk of his, I asked for some clarity. I told him I had never named a violin "The Messiah", and that if he was referring to my violins being worth millions of imperial lire, someone must be exaggerating. He told me that I had, in fact, made a violin called "The Messiah" and that it was one of the most expensive instruments in the world. He mused that maybe I hadn't made it yet, or maybe I haven't named it, but that it was true, because he had watched it on this glowing tube box of his.

Although the man seemed to be talking complete nonsense, he had such conviction and honesty in his eyes. He also seemed rather out of place. It was then that I fully noticed his attire. He was wearing a shade and cut of fabric that I cannot recall having ever encountered. His trousers were a speckled blue, and they seemed thick yet malleable to the shape of his body. The closest I have seen of it is by the docks, covering the cargo and whatnot, I don't know its name. If only you had been there, my boy!

Anyway, the rest of his attire was mostly hidden by an English jacket of some sort, nothing out of the ordinary, and he seemed reluctant to explain how he came to know more about my work than I was aware of. Feeling rather silly, but too fascinated to resist, I asked if he was talking about the future.

"Oh yes," he answered, "for all the good it seems to do me, I am from the future," he stated without even a blink or telling rub of the nose, "and you are a very famous man who lives on through his instruments. I probably shouldn't say, but then no one gave me a rule book, so I don't care. From the little I know, no one else can ever quite replicate what you made: the tones and suchlike. Quite brilliant, I think. Your voice lives on, Stradivari."

I was rather touched by this oracle. Forgive an old man for being intrigued by fools who would flatter him, but I cannot impress upon you the conviction with which he spoke. It was like an afterthought to him, a casual remembrance, as if recalling the name of an old acquaintance for an after-dinner anecdote, and being pleased to have grasped the detail. It was convincing.

Now before you buy me passage to the madhouses of San Servolo, let me tell you what happened next. The man, sitting relaxed as he was by now, bent over the table as if suddenly afflicted by a bad dose of *agita*. I helped him to his feet, asked what was the matter and shouted for water, but he simply said "It's happening again. It's getting shorter each time."

"What is happening again?" I asked.

He clutched at my arm. "I can see now, before I arrive. I am floating around glass boxes in space. But not space up there," he strained a finger to the sky, "the space between moments. I can't control it. I can watch stars move. I hear the cries of man and beasts. I hear you, too, I think, in this place, I heard your violins playing. I hear a name between it all. I need to find him."

"Find who?" I asked, but the stranger threw my supporting hands away and turned to run. He left the cafe and rounded the corner, and I took off after him. Not that I expected to catch him, not with my old legs, but I felt I must try. Then there was a flash, as if lightning had struck. It made me shield my eyes without a thought, it was so bright. Just moments after he had left and I had reached the piazza, he was no longer there.

Your first thought, as was mine, would be that he made off around a corner, but unless he had forced entry to a dwelling, he had not the time to get far enough away. My eyes are not yet so old as my legs, I can assure you. He could not have reached a place to escape my vision in such a short span.

If I were being logical, I could fathom that, by some Chinese trick of powder, he had caused the flash, and that he did indeed have access to one of the nearby buildings. But for what reason? I was not robbed. I was not harmed. I have heard nothing of him since: in spite of extensive inquiry, no one has seen the Englishman in the bright blue trousers.

That is my tale. And I must apologise to have left it so long to tell you. I hope also this goes some way to explaining my distance at your last visit, for this encounter played on my mind in the most distracting way.

I could not shake the words he had said from my ears, like trapped water after a dip in the baths. He said that "my voice" would live on in my instruments, and, after some time and much thought, that is when I realised it. The warty wood of my latest creations that seems never to smooth out no matter how much I try? Remember? It is *my* voice! My voice has got old and strained, and rough. I could read the most beautiful Virgil, word-for-word, but it would not hold the vitality and passion I had when I read the same as a young man. The essence of me is draining away, as must we all, and with it, the less of me there is to imbue my works.

Our Lord gave me a gift. Is it a wonder, that he, a carpenter, would give such a talent of creation and resurrection in this way? I pondered on this, and decided to 'speak' with him through my instruments. There is one - I do not speak of this often, though I think you and your siblings may know, given my reluctance to let you near it - violin that has stayed with me for many years now. It was the violin that made me realise I was no longer an apprentice, and I kept it for both personal and practical reasons. It was this violin that I picked up, not two nights ago, and played in communion with God to get my answers. Imagine your mother's surprise, to hear me play, rather than the usual scrapes and knocks of my workshop in the rafters! I had told her, however, that under no circumstances should I be disturbed that evening.

It is hard for me to describe how the conversation went, my son, and I ask you to keep this letter and notion in good faith. I raised you to believe, but I never asked you to have faith before, please do so now, for your old father. The best way I can render what I heard that night, as the strings vibrated with my spirit of questioning, is written below. These words are crude, and it was a feeling more than anything else, so please excuse the rough edges.

I asked: will my voice live on through my creations? And this is what I heard in reply.

There is no such thing as silence, because of me. There is a noise behind everything, even on the quietest nights, when not even the insects or the wind are raising their voices. You can plug your ears, but there is no silence. One day, my children will find this noise. They will finally stop and listen for it, and they will believe they are hearing it for the first time. But it has been there always, ever since I broke the silence. And when they hear it, they will think, 'I know what that is, now it is there to be heard.' And they will be happy with themselves for having heard it, and believe that there is nothing else to know because of it. They will be wrong, but I do not blame them for it. Just like those who hear the same music a thousand times, yet never hear it enough, and on each listening discover something new and beautiful, and yet still believe that they know some truth but are mistaken, I will not blame them for not understanding. I cannot.

Something happened, and the world splintered, and music poured out of the cracks. And in it, there was your voice, and it lived on before and after you. You may think yourself special: you are not so, neither am I. But the sound. Without it, there is nothing, and that can't be. Your creations are themselves made from it, and in themselves make it close to purity again. They must be heard, and when they are, so will you be, my son.

I wrote this as quickly as I could move the quill, having broken from the trance of an open D string, barely touching the hair, quivering almost imperceptibly from my lightest touch, yet resonating as if in the great cathedral! The words were not given to me, I had to find them myself, and these were the best I could do.

Now my tale really does end, and, though I should fear you will think me insane in my old age, I trust you will trust me, that everything I have told you is true to the best of my belief, and that my belief, dear boy, is strong.

So you see why I am so happy. In both worlds I will live on. You will bring me grandchildren, no doubt, and they will carry our name. But more so, my instruments, they are out in the world, little parts of me, waiting to be played. Maybe one is being played right now, and somewhere I am singing, shaping the air into the existence of others, as if there myself, whispering fates.

I feel that an epiphany is not one that comes to the young, nor to those with long left in this world. Do not be sad, I will see you before I go, but you must heed these next instructions, just in case.

Of my instruments, although I know many are already scattered around God's good Earth, there is one, *the* one, that I wish to keep with me till the end. When that happens, it will of course pass to your brother Francesco. I know you and he don't have much to say to each other, and to you he must seem almost as old as I, but he will be taking it into his care. When he passes, it will pass to you, and so on, hopefully, to your children.

This matter is of no surprise, I'm sure, but this is what you must hear now. Play it! Play it, boy! It *must* be played. Do not let it linger in a forgotten chest, or hang it for decoration, it may as well be firewood in that case. For God's sake, play it or get another to play it for you. I fancy you may still remember your scales, but if you wish another to let it sing, let them conduct! And if you should ever part with it, or any other that is left, please be sure that it will be heard. Make it a condition, make the benefactor promise. And when you do play or hear it played, listen for me. I will be there.

In this way, I hope at least for the generations that we can influence between us to still have a voice in this world as I enter the next. When I go, I am going to find these glass boxes that the stranger spoke of, and listen for the sound that breaks the silence between them. Please help me, my son, to keep my voice in the world. I would hate for my work to become sealed away and looked at through a glass box of its own, unheard, silent. This is my wish. Let it be played: why else was it created?

I leave you now, Paolo, no doubt in a much different mind than when you began. If you ignore all else in this letter as the fever of an old fool, take heed of these last sentences, they are all that is important to me now. I have long provided the wealth and status to keep your mother and others supported for many years to come. In return, grant me this wish.

Visit soon, my boy, I think I have some time yet. May God keep you both safe and find you well in this delicate world.

Your loving father.

Garry Abbott

Garry Abbott is a musician and writer who lives in Staffordshire in the UK with his fiancée and two cats. 'The Dimension Scales and other stories' is his first self-published fiction collection.

To find out more about Garry's other work and future projects, please visit www.garryabbott.co.uk or connect with him on Twitter @Garry_Abbott.

Garry would like to thank the team at ProofProfessor (www.proofprofessor.com) for their fantastic copyediting service and Nicola Winstanley (www.nicwinstanley.com) for her excellent cover design.

Made in the USA
Charleston, SC
31 October 2016